The Lyin' King

Table of Contents

Chapter 1: The Struggle

Staring at the reflection of my naked body in the bathroom mirror, I contemplated the need of liposuction or exercise. Maybe even a few of those wrap thingys could work. I never desired to be a skinny girl; just thick in all the right places. Seems like a pretty reasonable request to me. I pinch the sides of my "love handles" together as if I were making my belly talk; the sound of my son scuffing his shoes across the hardwood floors ejected criticizing thoughts of the flaws in my curves from my mind. I quickly reached for my robe, as I forgot to teach my little Prince the politeness of knocking. He pushed open the door.

"Mama! Do I have to go to daycare tonight? Can't I just go to work with you??" He complained.

He stood there with both hands out in front of him as if he had just single handedly figured out a way to solve the daycare dilemma.

"Thias, can't is not a word! And no, you may not! What do you think you could do at work with me for eight hours???"

"I can help you clean toilets or vacuum!" He suggests, hoping he wouldn't receive another rebuttal. "But why can't?" he began, sucking his teeth attempting to correct himself.

"I mean, can we just stay home tonight?"

"Listen Pumpkin, you know I go to school during the day. I have to work sometime. Gotta pay the bills, baby. Now go put your jacket on and grab your blanket. I'm already late."

Trying to hide his disappointment, he pivots around on his right foot and slides out my room down the hallway. I know he wants to spend more nights with me; maybe watching cartoons on the couch, having a real dinner, or sleeping next to me in my bed instead of a mat on the floor. He knows I'm trying. My baby knows. My head began to ache, just a little. I didn't get much sleep after class today; trying to catch up on my paper that was due two days ago. I look over at the clock. It's nine twenty already! I grabbed my black Dickies and a thermal. Whoever said all black was slimming hasn't tried on a pair of Dickies. I grabbed a pair of non-matching socks and sat on the edge of the bed to put on my slip resistant workforce shoes. I began to lace them up when I see Thias standing by the door with his head leaning against the wall.

"Mama, what's that one going to be?"

"What one?"

He points to the easel that held a painting I had just started.

"I'm still working on that baby, but whatever it turns out to be, it's going to sell. I feel it. Once I get it out there, I'll have investors lined up to open up a gallery."

"But Mama, why don't you just sell these other ones?"

We both stood up straight and looked around the room. I never realized how many paintings I actually had.

"Baby, those aren't my best work." I replied, projecting my doubtful thoughts into an oh so receptive universe.

"How do you know mama, nobody's ever seen them but you?"

My kid had a point. I don't really know; just never had the gut feeling about any of them, I guess. I looked over at the clock again, nine thirty!

"Put on your jacket, let's go!"

Thias put on his jacket as I threw on my coat, grabbing his blanket before he forgot. I rushed down the hallway taking the keys and my phone off the counter and headed out the door. I could hear the sound of the bus coming to a stop in front of our building, as I frantically try to lock the front door.

"Come on Thias!! Run and catch the door!"

My baby boy took off like he was in a race competition. I wasn't far behind him. He jumped on the bus and waved at the bus driver, then headed towards the back to find us a seat. A few seconds later, I hopped up the steps. The bus driver looked at me and smiled; very nice old man, Mr. James.

"How you doing Mr. James, did Thias give you the bus fare?" I asked, knowing I hadn't given Thias any money. I'm just hoping he wouldn't notice that I was a horrible liar. The way he looked at me, I could tell he knew I didn't have any money or a bus pass.

"It's alright young lady." He looked over the top of his glasses. "I got you guys tonight, but I can't do this all the time."

"I understand Mr. James. God bless you, thank you."

I felt bad I had to lie. I just couldn't have my baby walking in this cold. I looked down the aisle of the bus; he had already found us a seat. I plopped down next to him. A little out of breath and head still throbbing, I closed my eyes to thank God for always making a way for us. Thias slid his fingers through mine and squeezed my hand.

"Mama, it's going to get better." he whispered, as if he knew I had just lied our way onto the bus. He knew. I'm sure he did. I looked him in his soft brown eyes, running my fingers through his big black curls with my other hand.

"I know sweetie. Mommy knows."
I told him I knew. I wasn't sure when it would get better. I knew I wanted better for us, I knew I was trying; but I didn't know when things would change. Soon I hope….things would change soon.

As we sat on the bus I kept my eyes closed, fantasizing about a different life for us. One where I owned my own gallery, and spent more time with Thias. The bus slowed down, preparing to stop right in front of the day care. As we walked down the aisle I held on tight to Thias's cold, fragile little hands, so he wouldn't fall over anyone in their seats. I thanked Mr. James again; he gave me a slight wave of acknowledgement as we stepped off the bus. I bundled him up and we ran across the street to the twenty-four hour daycare that he had been attending since I started this night shift gig. As we open the door, I notice the director still in her office. What is she doing here this late? I thought to myself. We scurried past like little mice trying to avoid a mouse trap. I know I hadn't paid for the week, I just needed a couple more days; that's all. We got to the classroom; his caregiver wasn't in there; just children lying down on mats. Some half sleep, others fighting their sleep. I kneeled down beside Thias taking off his jacket and putting his things in the cubby.

"Baby listen, try not to be too noticeable tonight ok? It's almost 10, so find a mat, lie down and go to sleep. Be a good boy for mama ok?"

"Ok mama." He leans over and kisses me on my forehead. He's so sweet, my baby boy. I'm still squatting at his cubby watching as he tries to find an empty mat. Finally he found an empty one, laid down, turned towards me and mouthed, "I love you mama". I nodded my head, giving him an, "I love you too Prince."

I stood up straight, stuffing the ends of my auburn locs under the back of my toboggan; attempting yet another great escape, without being seen. I held my head down and walked quickly towards the door. Forgetting the bells, I pushed the door open making a supreme amount of unnecessary noise. I looked over to the office, but no one seemed to notice. I rushed outside and stood there to bask in the feeling of relief. The universe was on my side tonight. I pull my phone out of my pocket to check the time. Man! Nine fifty-five! I still have a twenty minute walk to work. I noticed another bus pulling up. The thought came to mind, but I should probably walk. I've done enough sneaking around for one night. I stuffed my hands deep in my coat pockets and began heading towards Piedmont Ave, the wind beating my face with every stride. I could just feel my nose turning red. I began to think of the many reason I decided to move to Atlanta; warmer weather being one of them. It's moments like these that made me wish I had a car. If Shaun sees me coming in late again, he is going to have one of his dramatic bitch-fits. Not wanting to hear his mouth gave me a little pep to my step, but not as much as me needing this job. A few more blocks, that's all you got; trying to encourage myself to fight through this cold January air. Carter & Stone Development is just fifteen minutes away. Realizing that I had only been walking for five minutes, I decided to cross the street now to save some time later. I looked around to make sure no APD was in sight. Last thing I need is a j-walking ticket, Georgia loves to ticket somebody. The coast was clear. I stepped off the sidewalk; forgetting the number one rule to crossing the street. I could see bright lights out of my peripheral, but it was too late for me to react. As if that wasn't enough warning, the driver holds down the horn; startling me, sending me falling backwards onto the sidewalk. I landed on my back; staring off into the sky. I just laid there. Not that I was hurt. I just began to wonder ...*"Could this actually be my karma from all of my suspicious behavior tonight?"* There is no way the universe works that fast, right? Clearly, checking for APD did not include

looking for any other cars on the road.
Turning my head to the right to see a red,
midsize sedan going in reverse. I rolled
over, pushing myself on my knees to stand
up, brushing the dust off my hands onto my
pants and coat; purposely keeping my back
turned towards the street to avoid any
conversation with the busta who almost hit
me. I could hear the car come to a stop
behind me. People don't just do hit and runs
these days.
"I am soooo sorry, are you okay?" I could
hear the car door close.
 I rolled my eyes, tilting my head backwards
as I reluctantly turned around to respond.
"Yea sure, I'm fine. I'm alright."
He walked around the car onto the sidewalk.
"Miss Lady, I really didn't see you with all
this black on."
"Clearly, I didn't see you either." I replied
sarcastically.
I stood back to get a better look at him;
pretending to be getting myself together. He
was very short. I mean I'm 5'4, so he was a
tiny bit taller than me. By a tiny bit, I do
mean itsy; maybe 5'7 at the most. He stood
there, shoulders back, arms parallel to his
body. There was a demand in his stance. His
clothes were fairly dusty as if he had been
working in sand all day. His skin was a milk
chocolate complexion; very smooth. He had
tattoos going down both arms. All I could

think was, *"Where yo jacket fool?"* Must be warm in the car. I looked over at the car, the windows had dark tint and the rims were the same color red. He seemed a bit flashy at first glance. Well, his car was anyway.

I turned to walk away and he called out, "Wait a minute! Where you going?!"

Without turning around I threw my hand up and said, "To work! If I still have a job by the time I get there!"

Following close behind he said, "Let me take you please! That's the least I can do!"

"Did you not just hear me say I'm late? I don't need a ride! I don't even know you!" I replied in a very forthright tone.

"Woman, I'm taking you to work." he demanded. "I mean, I almost hit ya doggone tail!"

I raised my eyebrows looking him up and down, trying to figure out who he thought he was talking to; or better yet what grown man says doggone tail?

"I know you cold, stop being stubborn and get in the car......Please?"

I rolled my eyes again. So now he wants to be polite? I pulled my phone out of my pocket. Damnit! It's ten ten; still another fifteen minute walk versus a five minute drive. He does have a point. It is cold and he is the reason why I'm even later than what I would have been.

"Ok. I work right up the block at Carter & Stone."

"Thank you! You see how easy that was?"

I shook my head. "Don't push it." I snarled in my typical black girl with an attitude tone of voice. He smiled and all I could see was gold teeth. *"Oh my! I can't stand gold teeth; must be an Atlanta thing."* His smile was adorable though. And those arms! So strong..... Focus! You don't need those types of problems. I turned to walk back towards the car reaching for the door handle, and then our hands touch. A surge of energy transferred between us. That feeling had to have been....... Wait a minute, it's been awhile. I'm tripping. Snapping myself out of the sexually explicit thoughts that were trying to invade my mind, he moves my hand out of the way and said, "I got it."

I cleared my throat and stepped back. Very surprised I must say. He didn't look like the type to open doors. Nonetheless, I obliged his efforts. I sat down on the black leather seats, as he closed the door. It smelled good in there and surprisingly clean. I figured he'd have a lot of cups and fast food wrappings everywhere, but no it was clean. The old cliché "Never judge a book by its cover" came to mind. I watched him as he walked around the front of the car. It was something in his walk. It said something like, I'm short but don't push me. I giggled to myself. That was a good one. Seriously, it was something in his walk. I just can't put my finger on it. I reached over and unlocked his door. He paused for a second as if I had surprised him. No big deal, it's cold outside, right? Not that he seemed too bothered by it; with no jacket on and a shirt that muscle heads wear to show their arms off. I have to admit his arms were nice though. I might have said that already. He opened the door and sat down in the car. "

You aiight?" he asked with a bit of country grammar slang. I sat back folding my arms, sure to give him more of my attitude.

"Yea, I'm Alright!" I replied with emphasis on "alright", so he knows how to say it correctly.

"You hungry? I could stop and get you something to eat."

I looked at him with a side eye. My stomach saying, *"Of course we're hungry silly!"*, which was totally opposite of what came out my mouth. "Seriously? What part of late are you not understanding? All I need from you is a ride there and for you to learn how to drive."

He laughed, as if I were joking. I kind of was. This whole playing hard to get thing was never my strong suit. "Ok, you got it. Are you always this mean?"

Arms still crossed I looked out the passenger side window as if there were really a view for me to admire. "No, only when I almost lose my life and my job in the same night." I snapped back.

"Well that's life baby girl. You can't let that ruin your night though." he stated with a chuckle. "You're still here." A moment of silence, as he moved into ongoing traffic.

"What's your name beautiful?" I look over at him annoyed with all the nicknames he had given me within thirty seconds.

"Late!" I mumbled.

"Late huh? Well it's nice to meet you Late. My name is Arsen; but I go by Ace. I figure it's best you know who you riding with just in case I'm actually like a serial killer or something." he said laughing at his own jokes.

I do that too at times; I'm actually hilarious to me. I looked at him, as he looked straight ahead watching the road as if he was sure not to almost run over anyone else. "Serial killer, huh? That would make for an interesting night." I replied.

"I'm sure it would."

"Sage." I mumbled under my breath.

"What was that?" He replied with confusion.

"Sage, my name is Sage. Turn right here. I can walk the rest of the way."

"Sage, that's beautiful; but I am taking you all the way to work, just in case I decide to stalk you later?" he said laughing again.

"Hmmmm, if you insist." He continues to drive towards the front of my building.

We both sit there in silence. No music, no talking, just the sound of us inhaling and exhaling. He pulls up to the front door; I slowly pick up my purse and reach for the door. He pushes the lock button only unlocking his, jumping out and rushing to open my door. I tried to hide my smile from him. *"How cute."* I thought. I hesitate before getting out the car. Not sure for what reason, but I couldn't help but get the feeling that I had known him a lot longer than ten minutes. He stood there with the door open and with his hand extended to assist me out of the car. I declined his offer; trying to act as though his gentlemen like gestures didn't faze me, when inside I was full of butterflies. How incredibly lame, I know. I stood up and in that moment I caught a glimpse of his hazel eyes. They were so sincere and yet so sad. I had a foster mom that always said a person's eyes were the windows to their soul. If that were true in that moment, I felt something familiar about his.

"Thank you for the ride Arsen."

"Ace, you can call me Ace." he said correcting me.

I cut my eyes over at him and reluctantly gave in to his demands. "Thank you for the ride Ace."

He smiled as if he felt like he made tremendous progress from our first moments of meeting each other.

"Sage, I can give you a ride home in the morning if you need it?"

"No thank you. I teach my son not to ride in the car with strangers. Imagine what he will think if he seen you coming to pick us up?"

"You have a son, huh?"

"Yeah, is that a problem?" I was hoping his response would give me a reason to not want to ever see him again. Like an "I told you they were all the same" moment.

"Of course not! I can tell you're a good mom."

Damnit universe! Why is he saying all the right things?!

"Well, since you won't let me get you anything to eat..." he continued, "Here, take this and get y'all some breakfast in the morning." He reached in his pocket pulling out his wallet, handing me two twenty dollar bills. I pushed his hand away.

"No thank you. I have those same two twenties in my purse, we are fine."

Inside I knew that my son would have to walk home because I didn't have bus fare and we had no food in the house because I didn't get paid until Friday. Call it pride, but I couldn't accept that from him. In my experience, men don't just give you rides and feed your kids for free.

"Take my number then. Just in case you need a ride or something."

"No thank you! I will be fine Ace, as long as you don't try to hit me with your car again." We both looked at each other and smiled. He looked as if he wanted to say something else, I almost wanted him to.

"Williams!!!!" The sound of Shaun yelling my name interrupted whatever moment that I thought I was having with this stranger I had just met. Almost like a bubble burst over my head. "Williams! This is the third time this week you done got here late man!!!! You think you special or something?? What's going on? You out here cake baking when you need to be working!"

"Oh my goodness Shaun! I don't even...." Before I could finish my sentence Arsen took over.

"Sir, I am sorry she is late. She would have been on time, but I almost hit her with my car as she was crossing the street. Can you take it easy on her tonight? It's not her fault." His grammar got proper real quick. I thought to myself, Bravo Mr. Arsen, Bravo!!!! Shaun stands at the door with his arms crossed. "Yea well, tonight's the first night she got a legitimate excuse. Come on Williams get to work."

I looked at Arsen and gave him a silent thank you with my eyes. He smiled, showing all his gold teeth. Shaun turn around to head back inside, I ran up behind him to catch the door before it closed. I watched Arsen watch me as I locked the door behind me. He stood there as if he were making sure I was safely inside before he left. I wasn't sure if I was going to see him again, but it felt like we had already met many lifetimes before.

Chapter 2: Miss Williams

"Miss Williams....Miss Williams!" I could hear a stern voice struggling to say my name over and over again; each time a little clearer and angrier than the last. "Miss Williams!!!"

I started to come to, lifting my head up from the desk. My classmate next to me was nudging me with her elbow.

"Girl, get your phone." she said in a very low yet urgent voice.

"Miss Williams!"

I rub my eyes to clear my vision, swinging my locs out of the way, only to see my psychology professor standing over me with her faced extremely perturbed.

"Miss Williams, not only are you sleeping in my class, but you didn't bother to put your phone on silent. Both are extremely disturbing."

I straighten myself up, wiping the saliva from my mouth. I literally haven't slept in days. I couldn't afford to miss any more time in this class, so I borrowed an extra bus pass from Shelly at work last night. If only my professor knew what it took for me to even get here this morning.

"I apologize, Mrs. Lancaster. I didn't mean to disturb the class. I had a really long night last night." I responded sincerely.

"Yes, well I am not responsible for that. This is not high school Miss Williams; I do not babysit grown....."

My phone began to ring again, interrupting the professor in the middle of her sentence. Seeing how increasingly upset she was becoming, I quickly hit the silence button. She tapped her index finger on the corner of my desk, as to signal that as my last warning and walked away. I checked my phone to see who it was blowing me up. Five missed calls from my son's elementary school. Professor Lancaster sat down at her desk and I immediately stood up as if we were playing the "Bop the Weasel" game; only she and I were the weasels.

"And where are you going now, Miss Williams?" she demanded extremely vexed.

"It's my son's school, Professor Lancaster. I have to call them back...it seems urgent."

I didn't care whether she objected or not, I was going to the hallway to return this call regardless. She waved me off as if to say whatever. I hurried towards the classroom door and into the hallway. I dialed the schools number only to get a busy signal. Frustrated and concerned at this point, I attempted to call out again. Another busy signal!!! I hit the end button and my phone began to ring. I quickly answered.

"Hello? Hello?"

"Is this Miss Williams, Thias's mother?" I could hear the school counselor on the other end.

"Yes, yes it is. Is my baby okay? I was in class; I didn't know the phone was ringing."

"Ummm, yes Miss Williams. Thias seems to have a bit of a red eye; did you notice that this morning before he went to school?"

"Yeah, just a little." I replied, not really sure. I don't remember noticing anything out of place this morning.

"I picked him up from daycare this morning when I got off. I noticed it was a little red but I figured it was because he was just waking up. Why? What's the problem?"

"The problem is....Miss Williams., is that it seems to be because of a black eye. Maybe someone is hitting him?" she asked in a very cautious manner, as if she knew she could possibly strike a nerve with her statement. Suddenly, I felt extreme amounts of blood rushing to my head. Is this broad calling me to accuse me of beating my baby? Has she lost her damn mind?

"EXCUSE ME!?" I replied, transforming into Mama Bear mode. "Are you implying that my child is being abused? Where is my baby? Have you talked to him? He is old enough to tell you that he is very well taken care of and is far from living in a household of abuse. You know what? Don't worry about it! I am coming to get him right now."

"Miss. Williams, please calm down. I did not mean to offend you. It's standard that we ask these types of questions in this situation."

"Situation?" I interrupted. "What type of situation? My son doesn't get yelled at for Christ Sake! I will speak to you when I get there and I lay eyes on my son."

Not giving it a second thought I hung up the phone and rushed back into the classroom to grab my belongings.

"Miss Williams! Are you leaving?"

Taking in a deep breathe trying to calm myself before replying to this stuck up old hag, I turned around and calmly countered, "Yes Professor, I am leaving. My son needs me."

Turning to walk towards the door I hear, "His father can't get him? You can't miss any more time in this class or I will have to fail you."

I paused in my tracks. Tuh! His father, huh? I forgot an old white woman couldn't even phantom a life where fathers don't exist. She continued, "Miss Williams, you don't want to fail this class, do you?"

I think to myself, *"Is that a trick question? Of course not lady!"* Instead I looked her in the eyes from across the room and said, "No Professor, I don't; but I am more afraid of failing my son. Also, CAN'T is not a word". I looked around at my childless classmates, who seem shocked at my response. They couldn't picture making these types of sacrifices. I pushed open the door and walked out, being sure to let it slam as loudly as possible behind me.

    A million thoughts ran through my mind as I made my way out the school. I've always feared having someone tell me that I wasn't a good mother and that Thias would be taken and sent to a foster home. I mean I know I don't have everything, but I take care of him the best I can. I definitely don't abuse him. He is my life. I couldn't imagine my life without him. Social Services took me from my mother while I was at school. Granted she really was unfit and bat crazy, but nonetheless that is how they do; I know firsthand. Oh my goodness, I wouldn't be able to control myself if I get there and there is a social worker there trying to take my baby from me. I would flip, and possibly rag-tag her ass all the way back to her car. I had been so heated that I didn't realize I hadn't put my jacket on until I opened the door and the wind gave me a reality check. I dropped my briefcase on the ground to position my jacket and scarf. Looking over at the bus stop I could tell it was pretty crowded, but I began to head over trying to keep my mind from over thinking. As I get closer to the benches, I could hear vague chatter of today's weather and who saw what reality show last night. The only thing on my mind was getting to Thias. I leaned on the glass of the bus stop shelter, staring off into a daze thinking of every worst possible outcome of today.

An older lady that was sitting inside on the bench tapped on the glass to get my attention. She motioned for me to come sit beside her. I was very hesitant at first, but the look in her eyes made me feel guilty about declining. I maneuver my way through the small crowd with a couple of excuse me's and thank you's, sitting down next to her. I softly leaned over and gave her a thank you. She smiled. Somehow I ended up back into my whirlwind thoughts of what ifs? *"What if they try to take him from me? What if they think I'm abusing him? What if they think I'm an unfit mother?"* What if! What if! What if! Suddenly, the sound of the older woman's voice paused my erratic thinking.

"Whatever is on your mind baby, you have to give it to God." she said, tapping me on my knee cap.

"Oh, I'm fine ma'am." I replied. Not sure if I was trying to convince her or myself. She was right; I should give it to him. Only thing is, I'm used to fighting these battles myself. Many times I question his purpose for my life. It seems as though I was made for struggle and pain. She looked at me and smiled again; tapping my knee once more as if to reassure me that she knows what I am thinking. Luckily, the bus pulls up. I looked to her and offer my assistance with her bags. She hands me a couple grocery bags that were on the ground next to her. I wait for her to get on the bus first and I follow close behind. Sitting her bags in the seat next to her, I thanked her once again for offering a seat to her. I moved towards the back of the bus, hoping no one would follow me there. I just needed some space, to be alone in my own thoughts. I sat down close to the window, resting my head on the cold glass. Closing my eyes, I began to pray silently to myself. *"God...."I began, "You know I can't live without him, right? You know that I am trying my very best. Please don't let them try to take my boy from me. I'm giving it to you now, Amen."* I slowly open my eyes as if I had just literally held a conversation with God himself.

With every bump in the road and stop the bus made, my stomach grew tighter. As we pulled up to the stop in front of

Thias's school, I began to get lightheaded. I stood up, pinching the top of my nose with my index finger and thumb, squeezing my eyes together; trying to shake off the dizziness. I open my eyes only to find the old woman staring at me. She looked me in my eyes and nodded her head. I wasn't entirely sure what that meant but I gave her a nod back; turned around and reached for my briefcase and headed towards the exit. I got off the bus and stood there, scared to move. Afraid of what I might be walking into. Inhaling deeply, I mustered up some courage and began walking towards the building. Palms sweaty and head still a little light, I push the bell for the front desk to buzz me in. Pulling on the door, I could feel my breathing become more and more heavy. God please....just please. I walk up to the front desk secretary, she had her head down. I placed my briefcase on the counter and began, "Excuse me, I am Thias Williams mother, I need to see him." She looks up at me as if I had spoken a different language than what she understands.

 "Thias is in the nurse's office with the school counselor. If you have a seat, I can call her up to escort you back." "Ok sure that's fine."
I haven't eaten all morning but for some strange reason now, I felt like something was about to come up. I sat down in the

chair trying to keep my composure. My right leg began to shake uncontrollably, as it does when I am extremely nervous. Moments later I hear the sound of heels clacking down the hallway; like whoever was wearing them was on an absolute mission to get to where they were going.

"Miss Williams?" Man, if I hear my name one more time today. "Miss Williams?" I lean forward to get a better view of who it was behind the desk calling my name.

"Yes" I replied respectfully, trying to keep a cool head and remain reasonable.

"Come on back please." The voice was similar to the one on the phone, so I could only assume that this was the school's counselor. I quickly pick up my briefcase and follow her back. We walk into the nurse's office and Thias runs up to me and gives me the biggest hug. All of a sudden, seeing him made my heart so much lighter. "Hey baby, you alright? What's going on? Let mommy look at your eye."

I reach to pull his eyelid up to get a better view when I hear, "Miss Williams, I wouldn't make direct contact with his eye if I were you."

I turned my head, placing my hand on my hip ready to bark on this lady once more. "And why the hell not? He is my baby." I could have left the hell part out, but honestly this counselor was long overdue for a tongue lashing. "No offense, Miss Williams", she continued, "Thias has the pink eye and it's very contagious."

"The pink eye?" I repeated with a sigh of relief. I looked at him, and then back at her. "Ma'am, I basically just told my teacher to kiss my ass, because you called me insinuating that my child is being abused; all for me to get here and you tell me it's the pink eye? I seriously thought you all were up here trying to take my baby from me."

"Miss Williams, I do apologize. I didn't mean to offend you, but there are precautionary measures that we have to take. The ratio of children attending this school that is actually being abused is one out of nine. If you could just understand that my position is not at all easy." The sincerity in her voice made me feel extremely out of place for even wanting to whoop her ass when I got there. She has a job to do, true indeed; and at least I can tell she cares.

"You know you're right, I apologize. You're just doing your job." That was my weak attempt at trying to take back all the cursing I did to her.

"Yes mam Miss Williams. On another note, Thias will not be able to attend school or daycare for at least 72 hours. With a couple days of eye drops, it should clear up. As you can imagine, something contagious like that we can't allow the other children to get infected."

"Yes I understand." I agreed. A little frustrated because I definitely wouldn't be able to go to class for the next couple days while he's out of school, or work for that matter. I couldn't send him to daycare like that. I definitely cannot afford any time off from work. Not that Shaun would willingly give it to me anyway. I kneeled down beside Thias and gave him a kiss on the cheek.

"It looks like we are going to get to stay home for the next couple nights, huh Prince? His eyes lit up with excitement.

"Really mama?!!" he exclaimed. "All I had to do was get sick and now we can stay home?" Everyone in the room started laughing.

"Yea well, don't think about staying sick, Pumpkin. Mama still has to work."

I turned to the nurse and the school counselor, "Thank y'all, I really appreciate your help."

"No problem Miss Williams. We will see you Monday Thias. Enjoy this time off with your mom." she said smiling and patting him on the head. I began putting on Thias jacket and walking toward the side exit by the nurse office.

"So Mama, we gonna watch movies tonight? With popcorn and blankets?"

I giggled looking down at him as we made our way around to the front of the school toward the bus stop.

"Sure baby, what movie you wanna watch?"

"I don't know mama, I'll have to see when we....."

"Miss Williams!!!"

Thias was interrupted by the sound of someone calling my name, but this time it wasn't my professor or the school counselor. "Miss Williams!!!" they called out once more.

I turned toward the building's parking lot from where the sound of the voice was coming from. Thias stretches his arm out and points toward an industrial size truck.

"Mama, you know that man?" My eyes follow his finger and jogging towards us was the same man that almost hit me with his car that night before.

"No baby, I don't know him."

"But Mama he's saying your name and he's coming this way." Thias said with confusion. "You don't know him mama but I think he might know you."

"Yeah Thias I know of him. I don't really know him though."

"Mama but I don't understand." I grabbed Thias hand and pulled him to me as Arsen got closer. He was smiling from ear to ear and politely waving, like he had just seen someone famous or something. He finally reached us, looking down at Thias he says, "What's up little man?"

With the raise of one eyebrow Thias replies, "I'm not sure if you're a stranger or not. My mama said she knows OF you, but she don't know you." I smiled covering up my mouth with my free hand.

"It's ok Thias, you can tell him hi."

"Hi sir." Thias replied politely.

"Hey, so what's your name?" Arsen responds, squatting down in front of him with his hand out.

Thias gives him high five and says "Thias!"

"I like that name! Mine is Arsen."

"Arsen? What does that mean?" I quickly intervened.

"Thias, what makes you think it means anything?"

Arsen responded, "Because he's right! It does. It means "Strong King", little man. What does yours mean?" Thias looks up at me and then back at Arsen.

"I'm not sure."

"It's ok. I'm sure your mom has a meaning for it." He assures Thias as he stands up to acknowledge me. "Sage." he calls my name softly staring me in my eyes.

"Arsen." I replied. "What are you doing here?"

"Just bringing my niece some lunch. I'm glad I came." he responded. Just then the bus pulls up to the bus stop. I tug on Thias arm.

"Come on baby before we miss the bus!" I move toward the bus stop. Arsen grabs my arm.

"Sage, I can take you guys where you need to go." I paused, looking at him through the strands of my locs hanging in my face and then at the bus as the line gets shorter.

"I don't know you and you don't need to know where I live. We are fine on the bus."

"Well fine." He says, pulling receipt paper out of his pants pocket and scribbling on it with a pen he had in his shirt pocket.

"Please just take my number this time, and use it. I'd really like to get to know you." He stuffed the paper in the palm of my hand, folding my fingers closed as if to make sure I don't drop it. I looked over to the bus; the last couple of people were getting on. I stuffed the paper down in my jacket pocket. Before turning around to walk away I smiled and said, "Bye Arsen."

"See you later Sage." Thias and I began running toward the bus. We made it just in time before the doors closed. Heading down the aisle I found myself following Arsen with my eyes as he made his way back to what seemed to be his work truck. We sat down in the middle row and I was still staring out the window, surprised that I had seen him again. Thias looks up at me and smiles. "Mama I like him."

I frizzed up his hair and kissed him on the cheek. "Silly! You don't even know him."

Smiling, I looked out the window; secretly thanking the universe for yet another chance encounter.

Chapter 3: Maybe I Should Call

Thias had been out of school since that Tuesday and he had all weekend to feel better. He's been jumping off the walls and swinging from light fixtures with excitement, from all the time we've been able to spend together. Resting my back against the headboard of my bed, I watch as he tumbled back and forth.

"Mama?" he pants as he jumps. "I love being home with you."

I smiled admiring how much he loves just spending time with me. I thought of taking him to the movies today; but my check was a little short from missing a few days this week. He didn't seem to mind though. He's such an appreciative kid; just the little things matter to him.

"I love being home with you too."

"Mama?" he said once more. "Yes, love?"

"This girl in my class…." he began, "….Amber. She says her mom stays home all the time while her daddy goes to work." I look at him dreading where I know this conversation is going next.

"Okaaayyyy….." I respond, waiting for something more.

"That's it, that's all I wanted to say." He drops down beside me, resting his head on my thigh. I began running my fingers through his curls, twirling them around my finger. I never really had a conversation about how he feels about his...you know, Sperm donor. Although, I can't blame his father too much. We were both young and immature. The only difference is, I grew up after Thias was born. His father? Well, he still has a ways to go.

"Pumpkin? Is there something you want to talk to me about?" I asked, desperately hoping he would say no.

"Mama, I just think you work too hard, all by yourself."

I leaned over pushing his hair back and planting a kiss on his forehead. "Thias, you don't worry your little heart about how hard mommy works. That's what Mamas do. I will always work to take care of you, and there is nothing wrong with that, ok?" He lifts up and looks me directly in my eyes. "But Mama! That's not the way it's supposed to be. You're not supposed to be by yourself." His voice began to crack as if he wanted to cry. I could see the tears trying to form in the corner of his eyes.

"Pumpkin....Pumpkin." I said with a smile, grabbing both sides of his face, rubbing our noses together. "I'm not by myself, I have you. If I have nothing else in this world, I have you." Trying to end this conversation, I started a tickle match. He laughed and laughed, yelling out "OK MAMA! Ok OK OK!! Stop it!" I grabbed him giving him hug.

"Now go get your night clothes ready! I'll run you some water so you can play battleship in the tub!! Only for thirty minutes though, ok? You have school tomorrow!"

"Ok Mama!" He jumps off the bed onto the floor with a thump; running out the room yelling, "Captain Thias! Prepare for battle!!!!"

I held my head down trying not to cry, expecting him to come barging back in my room any minute now. I stood up heading towards the bathroom to start his bath water. My foot got tangled up in the arm of my jacket that was thrown on the floor while Thias was jumping on the bed. I started to chuckle. "If I had put it in the right place to begin with, I wouldn't have tripped", I scolded myself. It's funny how we fuss at our children for the same things we do. I bend over to pick up my jacket tossing it back onto my bed, when a piece of paper fell out. I pick it up, carrying it into the bathroom with me. I plugged up the tub running the water and adjusting the temperature, so that it is just right. I started to feel dizzy again. That's been happening a lot lately. I should probably drink more water, amongst other things that I'm not doing to take care of myself. I look over to the bathroom mirror. I could see my baby fat peeking out from the bottom of my t-shirt. I guess I could stop calling it baby fat now, Thias is almost seven. I shouldn't be using that as an excuse anymore. I sat down on the toilet, disgusted from looking at my midsection, waiting for the water to finish running. Thias runs in the bathroom completely naked.

 "Mama! I got all of my battle gear!!!" he warns, as he tossed each toy in the tub.
"Oh yea? Well, what about your after battle gear?" I asked, looking for his night clothes.
"I forgot mama!" he replied laughing.
"Don't worry about it, I'll get them." I stood up to walk out the bathroom. "Hurry up Captain, you only got thirty minutes and I'm timing you!" He laughed and jumped in the tub splashing around. I walked into his room to search for some clean night clothes. I opened my hand to reach for the drawer, and the paper fell again. I almost forgot I had it. I sat at the edge of Thias's bed and opened it. "Ace", it read, with a telephone number and a heart. I have had this number for almost a week! *"Maybe I should call."* I thought. *"What if he's busy and doesn't have time to talk? Even more important, what would I say? What if my situation is too*

much for him?" He might think I have too much baggage. Honestly, I really do. I'm just not prepared to give a man any time right now. I'm not where I want to be. I have nothing to offer. Maybe I shouldn't call. I couldn't bring anyone into my mess right now and expect them to actually want to stick around. I should wait. That's what I will do. I'll wait until I have my shit together and a little more stable. *"Damnit Sage! There you go again! It's not like he's trying to marry you. Just talk, right? You can talk. No, I should wait. I should wait to call".*

"MAAAAA!!!!" The sound of Thias screaming shook me. I dropped the paper and ran down the hall to my bathroom.

"What is it baby? What's wrong?"

He looks at me with his round eyes and grins. "I captured all the bad guys' mommy; I'm ready to get out."

I let out a big sigh with my hand over my chest. "Oh, well get out then silly! You nearly gave me a heart attack!" He jumps out the tub and I hand him the towel. I remembered that I never got his night clothes as I said, "Dry yourself off Pumpkin. I gotta run and get your clothes."

Pacing down the hallway I began to think, maybe I should call? Walking into his room I grabbed some PJs out the drawer, dropping the pants on the floor as I struggled to close the drawer. *"Got it!"* I said to myself, finally getting the drawer closed. Kneeling down I scooped up his pants, and there was the paper. I looked at it. Maybe I should. Kneeling down once more I grabbed the paper and headed back to my bathroom. Thias was standing there all wrapped up in the towel.

"I'm soooo tired."

Handing him his night clothes, I replied, "Well good! I don't have to fight with you to go to sleep then, right?"

"Not tonight, mama. Maybe tomorrow, but I'm tired tonight." I smiled, watching him throw on his PJs like he had somewhere important to be and was running late.

"Ok, come on let me tuck you in Captain!" Reaching for his hand, I walked him down the hallway into his room. He jumps in bed and pulls the covers over himself. I sat down beside him kissing his forehead then both sides of his cheeks. "Goodnight, Pumpkin. Sweet dreams." He looked at me holding his arms out wanting a hug. I lean in and he wraps his arms around my neck.

"You are the best Mommy in the world. I love you." he whispers in my ear.

"Awwww, thank you baby. Goodnight, I love you." I got up, turned on his spider man night light, and walked back to my room.

I laid down on my bed, opening up the paper once more....staring at the number. *"Should call?"* I asked myself. I look over at my nightstand where my cell phone was charging. I should.... I'm going to call. I reach over and grab my phone. Pulling up the dial screen, I began to enter in the numbers. 5...5....5. I stopped and erased them. Maybe I shouldn't. *"Call, Sage."* I tell myself. *"Call, what's the worst that could happen?"* I began to dial again, this time at a much faster pace so I wouldn't talk myself out of it. 555-473-0960, send. The phone begins to ring. Once, twice, three....

"Hello?" I gasped. I was hoping it went to voicemail; but it was him. I couldn't say anything. My mouth wouldn't move.

"Sage?" he said. I hung up the phone. How did he know it was me? My phone begins to ring. I look at the number. Oh my goodness! It's him. I took in a deep breath and answered, "Hello?"

"Sage? So you gonna call and hang up?" he asked. I could hear him smiling through the phone.

"I didn't..." I began to stutter. I don't know why he made me nervous. "I didn't mean to hang up. I just didn't expect you to answer the phone."

"Why wouldn't I answer? I've been waiting all week for this call."

He's been waiting all week, tuh! That made me smile, but I couldn't give in. "Why? I'm really not that great, you know?" I said sarcastically.

"You have to be great if I like you."
That's something people are "supposed" to say. I doubt he was sincere about it. Trying to maintain my mean girl persona he encountered when we first met, I replied, "You don't know me, Arsen. That was the polite thing to say, but I am a big girl. You don't have to be nice because it's the right thing to do."
"It is the right thing to do Miss Lady. I'm not going to be mean, because you're not used to someone being nice." he replied. I got quiet. What could I possibly say to that? "I'm glad you called me. What are you doing?" he asked.
"I'm lying across my bed; just put my son to sleep. What are you up to?" I asked trying to keep the conversation going.
"I was reading." he said. Oh! He reads, I thought to myself.
"Reading what?" "The Bible." he responds. He reads the Bible at that? There was a pause.
"Well, I didn't mean to disturb you. You can call me back if you'd like?" I suggested.
"Sage, it's fine. I want to talk to you."
"Oh ok." I continued. "So what is your religion?"
He exhaled as if the question struck some type of nerve. "Religion is man-made. I have

a relationship with God and an understanding of the Universe."

"Interesting." I replied.

"Oh yea? How so?" he asked.

"I mean that is an interesting concept, especially nowadays with everyone stamping a religion on what is right or wrong."

"I am not guided by what man's idea of who God is, and I don't need the validation of being a certain religion to solidify my relationship with God. Besides, it's really just a way people justify the twisted interpretation of the bible, by attaching it to a religion." he explained.

"Do you believe that prayer works?" I asked curious to get his opinion.

"I believe that prayer is a healer." he responded. "You asked that question as if you're unsure of the power of prayer?"

"I have a very painful past. I just doubt sometimes that God heard my prayers."

"You know what baby girl….that's life. Everything in it is beautiful, even in the pain. That's when lessons are best learned. And this journey is all about growth for your soul."

Listening to him talk about life was refreshing. He was so hopeful and believed there to be more to life than the present moment. I couldn't imagine him ever being this deep when we first met. I guess I was quiet for too long, when he asked, "What are you thinking?"

"Nothing, just reflecting. I like the way you think Arsen." He laughed.

"You like the way I think? Well that's good to know. What do you like to do? In your free time?"

"I don't do much between school, work and Thias. I don't even paint as much as I used too."

"Paint?" he asked with excitement.

"Yes, I'm an artist. Well aspiring artist. I guess I won't be considered an artist until I actually sell my work."

"No, you are an artist. It's already in you. It's all about how you see yourself." I smiled.

"Are you always this positive?" I asked.

"Where I came from in life, that is the only way to be."

We continued our conversation for hours. This did not feel like the first conversation we ever had. It was so familiar to me. The laughing and minor debates about life, the flow of energy felt as if we had been here before. I'm not sure when or where, but this can't be the first time our souls have crossed paths. My phone began to beep. "Damnit! My phone is dying."

"I don't want it to end either." he said. I smiled. That's exactly what I meant.

"I can call you tomorrow." I suggested.
"Do you have class in the morning?" he asked.
 "No, I've sort of been dropped from this class. So I won't be back in school until next semester." I replied, completely forgetting the little spat I had with my professor last week.
"There's somewhere I would like to take you tomorrow, if you don't mind spending the day with me?" *"Uh oh!"* I thought to myself. *"Were just supposed to talk, Sage. I can't go anywhere with him, then it would be like a date."* "If it makes you feel better, we won't call it a date. I just want to show you something I think you might like." He insisted, almost as if he heard my thoughts.
"Well, I have to drop Thias off at school by 8:30. I still don't think you should know where I live so you can pick me up from there if you don't mind?"
"That's fine with me, whatever makes you comfortable."
"Ok then, see you in the morning?"
"Yes. Goodnight Sage." "Good night Arsen." We both began to laugh as neither of us had the courage to immediately end the call.
"Ok, seriously." I managed to get out through my laughter. "I'm hanging up now, goodnight."

"Goodnight beautiful." he replied.

I smiled and hit the end button. Resting on my back and looking at the ceiling, I couldn't help but think about seeing him again. He's completely different than what I expected and I couldn't wait for morning to come.

Chapter 4: Dancing In The Rain

Beep....Beep...Beep....Beep....! Rolling over to hit the snooze button on the alarm, I felt extremely tired. I was up all night on the phone not considering the consequences I would have to face in the morning. It's seven o'clock, maybe twenty more minutes wouldn't hurt. I considered staying in bed a little longer and what affect it would have with me getting Thias to school on time. No I should get up now, not to mention I have no idea what Arsen has planned or what I am going to wear. I hadn't been anywhere in a long time that required me to wear something other than black Dickies and a thermal. I was kind of excited; excited and exhausted. I dragged my way into Thias's room. I had to laugh, because he was halfway in and halfway out the bed; reminding me of why I had to stop him from sleeping in my bed.

"Hey man! Wake up! Time for school." I said as I tickled the bottom of his feet. He began to moan and whine as if he was too tired to move. "Come on; come on, up, up, up!!!" I yell, just to irritate him a little more. He slowly began to maneuver his way out the bed as I'm picking out his uniform for school. "When you finish getting dressed, go and brush your teeth, ok?"

"Ok Mama." he agreed.

For some reason, I have a little boost of energy; not sure where it came from. Maybe it's the anticipation of actually doing something other than work. Who knows, but I'm going to run with it today. I walk into my room towards the closet; standing there with the door opened staring as if something was going to magically put itself together and say, "Wear me! Wear me!" Man, I wonder if I should wear a dress. Probably not, it's the end of January. I'd look pretty crazy walking around in a dress in this weather. I don't think I should wear anything too fancy. *"Gosh! I hope he is not one of those guys who think going to the gym is a date; although I need to go. I just hope whatever the activity is, it doesn't require tennis shoes."* Jeans! Jeans are universal; they could go with any activity. I go to the back of my closet to pick out a pair of my most form fitting, curvalicious jeans. Not that I'm trying to be sexy for him or anything. I would like to clean up nice today, since he's only ever seen me in work clothes. I pull out a pair of light pencil leg jeans and a tan long sleeve, v neck shirt. I'll wear my brown boots and brown leather jacket to match, I thought to myself. Thias comes running in the room.

"Mama! I'm ready!" Looking at the clothes that I just laid out on the bed, he raises his eyebrows. "Mama, you never get dressed like that to take me to school. Where you going?"

"I don't know yet Pumpkin." I said with a smile. Knowing that sometimes my son tends to want to act like my father, I changed the subject. "Baby, go get you a banana and a glass of milk. Watch some cartoons until Mommy finishes getting dressed, ok?"

"Ok Mama." He skips out the room into the kitchen. *"The bus gets here at 8."* I thought to myself. I have enough time to shower and put a little makeup on. I jumped in the shower and hit all the "hot spots." Don't act like you've never done that! Neck, underarms, V-Box, and butt. Yes, I know. I stepped out to dry off. Standing in the mirror, I attempt to tie up my locks just to keep them out of my face for the day. A little mascara and eyeliner with rose color Matte lipstick. Hmmmm, I haven't done this in a while. It feels good to make myself pretty. Thias began to yell through the bathroom door. "Mama!!! It's seven forty-five!!!"

"I know Pumpkin!" I yell back. "I'm coming!" I hear him skip his way out of my room again. I open the door and began putting on the attire I had just picked out.

After putting on my socks and boots, I slid on my leather jacket and went to the mirror to check myself out. You clean up nice, Sage. You clean up nice! Looking down at the counter full of perfume and thought, *"I want to be sweet today,"* I pick up the sweetest smelling fragrance there and began to spray. Walking out the bathroom I grab my purse, my phone and head towards the door. Thias sees me coming down the hallway and he begins to smile.

"Mama you look so beautiful. I like when you look like that."

"Is that right? You gonna give ya mama a big head boy!" We both began to laugh.

I grabbed the keys off the counter and both our umbrellas from the vase at the door. They say it's supposed to rain today. I don't particularly like standing at the bus stop on rainy days, but luckily for us it hasn't started yet. I looked down at Thias putting his book bag on. He grabs my hand as we began to walk down the stairs and to the bus stop. We literally made perfect timing. The bus pulled up as soon as we got there. As we step on the bus, I began to get butterflies in my stomach. I know I'm completely over thinking it, I overthink everything. We sat down as the bus heads to the next stop. This is going to be the longest 15 minute ride in my life.

"Mama, I spy something brown."
Thias began wanting to play the I Spy game.
"My jacket?" I replied.
 "Why do you always guess right on the first try? It's your turn."
"It's called Women's Intuition."
"Woman what?" he asked.
"It's what us Mama's have. It's nature baby. Ok so my go?"
"Yep!" "I spy something blue. I'll give you a hint, it's inside the bus."
"Mama!!!" he whined. "Everything on the bus is blue, that's not fair!"
"Well just start naming stuff Thias. You're sure to get it right sooner or later."
"But not on the first try like you!" He complained.
"Ok, Ok....I'll do something else. I spy something........green."
He places his index finger on his chin and began to look around as if that would help him think a little harder. "Oh! I know, I know!!!" he shouted.
"What is it?"
"That lady's purse!" he exclaimed, pointing at the older lady's purse sitting in the middle of the aisle.
"That's right! You got it on the first try! See, I knew you could do it."

The bus began to slow down as we approached the stop in front of Thias's school. "Ok my turn! Last one!" he shouted. "Ok well let's do this one off the bus; we're at your school." We head towards the exit and down the steps. "I spy something red, a lot red!" he said.

"Hmmmm, is it the fire hydrant?"

"Oh wow mommy! This is the first time you never got it on the first try!"

"Really?" I asked. I was kinda of disappointed in myself, this never happened when we play this game. "Well what is it then?"

"That!!!" Thias raised his arm point at the red car with the same color red rims. My heart dropped.

"It's him." I said aloud, only meaning to keep it as an inner thought.

"That's who Mama?" As we were walking toward the parking lot, the driver door opened and Arsen stood up. "Hey!!!!" Thias began waving at Arsen. He smiled and waved back. We stopped at the car.

"Good morning Thias!" "Good morning beautiful!" Arsen acknowledged us.

"Good morning" I replied. "I'm going to take him in the school. I'll be out in a minute, ok?"

"Ok. I'll be right here." he said smiling.

We started walking toward the school as Thias turned and waved saying "Bye King!" Arsen waved back. I looked down at Thias, "Baby, his name is Arsen."

"I know Mama, but it means Strong King." I smiled and shook my head, ringing the bell to be buzzed in the front door. My stomach began to knot up again. I don't know why this man makes me so nervous. "Mama, I can walk the rest of the way." Thias assures me as we walk pass the front desk.

"You sure you don't want me to walk you to class?" I asked.

"Hey Thias!!!!" I could see a pretty girl with two puff ball ponytails running towards him. "Yeah Mama, I'm sure." he said very quickly. The little girl grabs his hand and they begin to walk down the hallway. He turns back to look at me and waved. I waved back. *"Ummmm hmmm. We are going to have to talk about her when he gets home."*

As I was turning to walk back out the front door, I could feel the butterflies getting stronger. *"I'm too old for this."* *I thought to myself. I really need to* "man up," *or in my case* "woman up." Coming through the glass double doors, I could see Arsen standing at the passenger side door. He already had it opened, waiting for me with one hand behind his back. The closer I get to the car; I'm feeling a little more at ease.

"You ready?" he asked, pulling a bouquet of flowers from behind his back.

"Oh wow! These are beautiful! Thank you!" I said with excitement. I can't remember the last time I got flowers. Hell to be honest, I don't even know what type of flowers they are. They weren't roses. It didn't matter because they truly were beautiful and a very thoughtful gesture. Before I had known it, I wrapped my arms around his neck to give him a hug. He paused before embracing me. His arms....it was something familiar about his warm embrace. He gently grabbed my arms, pushing me softly back to look me in my eyes. He felt it too. He leans over kissing me gently on my forehead. Surprisingly, I accepted. *"I don't even know him."* I thought. I don't know what this that I feel, but we've been here before....him and I. Snapping out of what seems to be a trance; I turn to get in the car as he gently closes the door behind me. I lean over to open his door. I hadn't realized I did, it was like an automatic reflex or something. He gets in and looks at me before starting the car.

"What?" I ask, turning up my nose.

He smiled and softly replied, "Nothing."

As we began to leave the parking lot I ask, "So where are we going?"

"You'll see."

I was ok with that response. I didn't mind not knowing. Sometimes the best moments

in life are surprises. I began staring out the window, as I sometimes do while I'm on the bus; getting lost in my thoughts. We turn down the ramp to enter the interstate. Traffic was extremely backed up. Looking over at the clock, I said, "It's about that time."
He laughed aloud replying, "Yes, the traffic is the only thing I can't stand about this city." "You mean other than the fact that it is becoming increasingly overpopulated. The ultimate moving destination for anyone looking to forget their past." I said sarcastically. Then in a quiet and sincere voice, "Reminiscing on my past." I said. "That's why I moved here anyway."
I could see him staring at me out the corner of my eye; he then says "You don't have to run anymore." Somehow I felt the sincerity in his voice, but I couldn't help but push that feeling to the side with thoughts of how many times I've heard some of things he was saying. I just didn't get why I felt the need to trust him, to believe his every word; I did. Maybe I was being way too vulnerable, but I didn't want to fight it. I wanted to give in.   Pushing our way through traffic, we continued with small talk of our favorite foods, colors, and vacations we would like to take. His smile...it was so adorable. Sometimes I caught myself laughing only to stop and stare at his profile as he was driving. God, it was something

about him. Something in those hazel eyes drew me in closer and closer. He began to exit the highway. I wasn't sure where we were at and still had no clue as to where we would end up.

"I hope the sun stays out for at least the next couple of hours." he said.

"Yeah, it is kind of nice out. They did say it was going to rain......", pausing to absorb my thoughts as I just realized what he said.

"Wait a minute, are we going to be outside?"

"Yes, you don't like being outside or something?" he said jokingly.

"Well I guess it depends on what we are going to be doing."

"Oh relax, you're going to love this." he replied as we were pulling into Piedmont Park. *"So we got a little park action."* I thought to myself. That's cute, kind of typical for the first date; but cute nonetheless. We find parking; he grabs a handful of nickels and dimes from the center console, and gets out to feed the meter. He comes to my side to open the door, holding out his hand. This time I accept. We began walking down the sidewalk towards the grass area of the park, when his phone began to ring. He puts the earpiece from his headset in his ear, "We are on the way down now.", and then quickly ended the call. I stop in my tracks, confused. "So are we having a double date or something? Who are we meeting? What are we doing?" I began asking questions one after another, not giving him any real opportunity to answer. He turns to me and began laughing at my spoiled like behavior.

"This isn't a date Sage, remember. I just want to show you something." Still a bit skeptical, I cross my arms and continue to stand still. He takes a couple steps back, gently unfolding my arms and holding one of my hands in the middle of both of his. Looking me directly in my eyes as if he were putting me under his spell he said, "Sage? Trust me." Again, in that moment I felt weak, and without my conscious permission my legs began to move. We continue walking onto the grass as we came to the top of a slight hill.

There was a plaid blanket laid out perfectly, with a basket and rose petals. Directly behind the blanket were two easels with blank canvases and stools. There stood a little Asian lady with a white painter's jacket and hat to match holding two pallet cheese trays in both hands, grinning from ear to ear. In shock, I dropped my purse and ran to canvases; running my fingers down, feeling the material.

"Textured canvas, these have to be like 48...."

"48 inch by 38inch." Arsen replied finishing my thoughts.

I look over at him with his arms crossed, as if he were admiring my happiness. "This is amazing Arsen! Can I paint on this?" asking permission as if I was a school aged girl in art class.

"Of course you can! This is all for you!"

I look over at the Asian lady who was still standing there smiling. Reaching out, she handed me one of the cheese trays. Arsen walked over to sit at the other easel.

"I have to be honest," he said "I'm no artist." I smiled looking down at the colors that were already on the color tray. "It's ok, it will still be beautiful."

Looking around, I admired how beautiful and peaceful this all was. The air was a bit cool and the sun was still peeking out through the clouds. Typical Georgia weather. This has to be the sweetest, most romantic setting I've ever been in. Arsen began to chuckle.

"These colors are so.....so normal." he said looking down at the artist trays.

"That's because you have to mix the colors to make other colors." I explained. "You know like how it was in art class at school?" I stood up and placed my color tray on the stool, to demonstrate. "Look, yellow and red makes orange." I said, guiding his hand with the brush, mixing the colors on the tray.

"Do I have to get another brush for each color?" he asked.

"No, no no." I covered my mouth as I giggled. "Usually I don't mix the color until I'm ready for it. And when I'm done I just dip the brush and mix another color if I need to." I explained. "Here, I'll show you on my painting."

I sat back down, pulling off my jacket and laid on the ground behind me. Taking in a deep breath as to absorb the positive energy around me, I looked at the space in between the two easels. There was a perfect view of the sun and the skyline of the trees. I began to paint, humming in between each stroke of my brush. The brush just danced across the canvas. I had no control, just freedom. I could feel Arsen watching me, which gave me even more confidence. The peace that I get from creating is so indescribable. I can feel the energy flowing through my body onto the canvas with every lift of my hand. Arsen stood up walking over to the picnic blanket to converse with the Asian lady. After speaking briefly, she began to walk away, but not before sending me a wave with the smile she kept the entire time we had been there. I gave her a nod and politely waved back with the paint brush. Arsen walks over to me. "Would you like to take a break? I got us some breakfast."

"Yeah sure, I'll be over there in a second." He turned around heading back towards the blanket as I stood up, placing the paint tray and brush down on the seat of the stool. I began to brush my hands together while walking toward Arsen. "Have a seat," he said with his hand stretched towards the blanket. I sat down, he followed. Opening the basket he began to take out a fruit salad, yogurt, bagels and cream cheese. Oddly enough, I'm thinking there would be fish, grits and cheese eggs in the basket. Although, I couldn't imagine it being in the basket that long and being warm. I like bagels. He had my favorite kind, cinnamon and raisins.

"This is nice. I never imagined having a morning like this." I said with a smile. He began spreading the cream cheese on a bagel. "You deserve many mornings like this, and so much more. I'm surprised no one has ever done anything like this for you?"

"No. The men I've picked haven't exactly been the romantic or thoughtful type." I replied. "Well, I'm glad you didn't pick me, I picked you." I began to smile, this time without covering my mouth. "Sage?" he says handing me the bagel he just prepared.

"I want to see that smile every day for the rest of my life."

I looked at him, I believed him. For the first time in my life I didn't question someone's intentions for me. I felt a chill run through every fiber of my being; staring at him in those sad hazel eyes. I believed him. Just then, a few rain drops began to fall. As moments passed the rain drops got heavier. I began to scream.

"Oh my goodness! Everything's getting wet!!!" As I was panicking, Arsen stood up grabbing my hand and pulling me out into the open grass.

"It's okay! Sage!"

The rain began pouring harder as we stood there. It was warm, as the drops hit my face with a slight breeze of the wind. I could see people running around us trying to find shelter. We just stood there, with his arms holding onto my waist, staring at each other. "It's okay! Sometimes in life you just have to dance in the rain." he said. "It's okay."

I was speechless. Everything about this moment was from a fairy tale; from the way that he held me, to the perfect sound of the rain falling. I could feel his lips getting closer to mine. I began to close my eyes and allowed our lips to meet. Everything in that moment was perfect, even in the rain.

Chapter 5: Step-Daddy

"Hey girl! Tanya shouts from the hallway, trying to over talk the vacuum. "So, how was ya date with ya little friend?" she asked, in a nosey yet envious type of way. "Oh girl it was good. It was really good." I replied, trying to down play how I really felt. I really wanted to say it was the most amazing romantic thing I've ever experienced in my whole adult life; but I and Tanya are not friends or even associates. Hell, the only reason why she knew about it is because her nosey ass was ear hustling when I and Shelly were talking about it. What even makes her think she could ask me about it? I don't know. I couldn't help but look at her quick weave that had hella glue and tracks showing. "Girl, that's it? He ain't spend no bread or throw you a couple hunnit?" she inquired further. No Bonquiqui, he did not throw me a couple hundreds and it was not that kind of date. I know she is used to her dates ending with a hundred on the dresser.

"Tanya, I had a good time. Thanks for asking." I politely responded, as I put my headphones back in and turned on the vacuum cleaner. Maybe she will get the hint, I giggled to myself. Nosey people. Pandora was making a sista feel real good tonight. Playing all the right songs that reminded me in some way of how Arsen makes me feel. I vibe my way through cleaning one office, gather my cleaning supplies to go to the next. I couldn't stop thinking about that date and Arsen's soft lips. I would love to feel his lips all ov....My phone began to vibrate interrupting my song and my thoughts. Shelly walks in the office.

"Ohhhh, who is that calling with a SILK ringtone?" she laughed. I smiled and held up one finger as I answered the phone.

"Hey Ace! Why are you still up?" I asked, not that I cared. I'm glad he chose to call me at two in the morning.

"I was thinking about you. I hate that you have to work night shifts like this. You should be home." he said, almost as if he had been thinking about this all night. He sounded real worried.

"Awww, Arsen you sound like you care!" I said jokingly.

"I do care love. I do."

"I'm a big girl. Besides sometimes you have to sacrifice until you get to where you need to be, right?"

"No, you shouldn't be sacrificing anything." he said quietly. "Listen, I know you're working so I don't want to keep you too long. You know Valentine's Day is this Friday and I wanted to make sure you didn't have any plans."

"Well I don't have any plans, but wait a minute, are you asking me to be your Valentine's Mr. Robinson?" He started laughing. "No, I'm asking you to be mine?" There was a brief pause. I didn't know how to take that. Like, was he serious? No, of course not. He couldn't be, right? "Yes Sage." he said, interrupting my thoughts again as if he knew that I was overthinking that statement. "Yes, would you be my Valentine?"

"Yes!!!!!" I shouted as if he just asked me to marry him. "Yes, Yes, Yes!!!"He began laughing again.

"Ok then, I'll start planning. Goodnight love"

"Goodnight, King." I could tell he was smiling. I was too.

"Girl, y'all sound like y'all a couple!" Shelly exclaimed. I almost forgot that she was standing there.

"Oh, no! He's just really sweet and thoughtful, you know?"

"Ummmm hmmm, yeah I know! I'm happy for you though Sage. You can't be afraid to -love someone again because of what you been through."

"Crazy! Who said anything about love?" I replied sarcastically. She looks me up and down with a side smirk on her face, turns to walk out the door and says,
"Your face. It's written all over your face child!"
I rest my cheek in the palms of my hands, as if I was going to feel what was written there. I smiled and shook my head. Could it be? I thought to myself. Could this be how it feels to fall in love?

I finished out the rest of my shift in such a good mood. I head to the break room to clock out. My girl Shelly was there, and so was Tanya.
"Sage, I'm going to catch some breakfast you want some?"
No girl, I'm good. I have to pick Thias up from daycare and take him to school."
"Damn! I keep forgetting! I wonder if I would be this thoughtless still when I have children." she said jokingly.
"Probably so!" I responded laughing. "I'm just kidding. It changes when you become a mother. It's almost like instinct. You just don't want to do the things you used to." I explained thinking back on how Thias has changed me as a person.
"Girl bye! With all that! You think I'd let having kids stop me from doing me?" exclaimed Tanya. Shelly and I both looked

at each other, and almost in perfect harmony we replied

"Of course YOU wouldn't Tanya." This girl is an absolute mess. Five kids and four baby daddies? Something should have stopped her from doing everybody else. I laughed to myself; but let me not be judgmental. She clearly has other issues. I grabbed my coat from the locker room, and headed out the door to the elevator.

"I'll see you Sunday night Shelly!"

"No you won't!!! I won't be back until Monday night! Hahaha!!"

"Oh, I see you girl. I'm about to enjoy these next three days off myself!" I laughed stepping onto the elevator.

   I stood there pushing the button to the ground floor feeling a bit tired; but happy that I'm going to be able to rest for the next three days. I wonder what Arsen is planning for Valentine's Day. I don't think anything can top our first date. Even if it wasn't anything extravagant, I would still want to just be in his presence. What do you get a man for Valentine's Day? I haven't had a Valentine in years. I'm not even sure if I'll have the extra money to get him anything. I can't come empty handed. I wonder if it would be lame of me to paint him a picture. I have to find something to do; I only have 2 days to plan really. The elevator stops and the doors open. I walked towards the door past corporate professionals that were coming into work. Some looking as though they wanted to turn around and walk out the building with me. I got to thinking how I don't want to work for someone else for the rest of my life. How great it would be to wake up and do something that I love and still be able to provide for Thias with no worries. I opened the double doors headed outside and the warmness of the morning sun hit my face. The air was a little cool, but it was light and flowing. I closed my eyes burying my hands down in the pockets of my coat, taking in a deep breath. In that instance, I could literally feel the weight of the world lifting off my shoulders and the universe saying to me; it was all going to be alright. Just then, my phone rang....Silk. That was the ringtone I had chosen for him, "More" was the song; only after that first date of course.

"Hello?"

"What are you thinking about?" he said.

"Huh? Nothing. What you mean?" I said extremely confused.

"Your eyes were closed." he replied. How did he? I looked toward the street and there it was, that red car; waiting on me as if it were a horse and chariot.

"Oh I see, you've come to give me a ride?"

"Well what kind of man would I be if I allowed my woman and son to walk in this weather?"

"Your woman? And son?" I asked.

"Wishful thinking, Sage. God said claim it, right?"

"That he did, Arsen." I replied hanging up the phone and walking toward the car. He leans over to open the door. I sit down and reach to give him a hug. "Thank you. I really appreciate this." He smiled and began driving.

"I know you might be a little tired today, so I wanted to take little man to school. Maybe after you get some rest and Thias gets out of school, we can all go to Skyzone this evening. I think he would like to jump around in there for a while. What you think?" Look at him, being so thoughtful towards my child too. He can't be real. Most men would meet a woman and just focus on getting in her pants, not even thinking of her child. He's so different; it's something about him. "Yes, Thias would love that! I would like to surprise him though. We haven't done anything like that in a while."

We pull up to Thias daycare and I get out to get him. He didn't have his school clothes on as usual. So I rushed him to the bathroom to change his clothes.

"Mommy, I don't like sleeping on that mat. It makes my neck hurt when I wake up." he complained.

"Ok sweetie. I will ask your teacher to let you sleep on two mats instead of one. It should make a difference, ok?"

"Ok mama."

I zipped up his jacket and we head outside. Thias notices Arsen's car and he lit up! He dropped my hand and ran towards the car where Arsen stepped out to open the back door. They shook hands and Arsen helped him into the car putting his seatbelt on.

"You ready for school little man?"

"Not really! My back hurts! And I didn't sleep good last night." He complained again. Arsen and I get into the front seat. "Well, why is that?" he asked.

Before Thias could continue on with his tangent I interrupted, "Those mats that they sleep on at daycare aren't really meant for a full night's sleep, you know?"

"Well is he allowed to bring his own mat?"

"I'm pretty sure he is. I've looked into it before but they were way out of my budget." I replied trying to hide the embarrassment of not being able to get my son everything he needs.

"Oh ok."

Thias and Arsen continue on with their conversation of the all the black inventors that didn't get their fair share of recognition. Thias's class is discussing black history month. We pull into the school's parking lot. We made it there early since we didn't have to take the bus. The administrator was out opening the doors for children being dropped off. Arsen pulls up to the door, and the teacher opens Thias door.

"See you later Pumpkin. Have a good day baby."

"See you this afternoon little man!"

"Cool! You're picking me up Arsen?!" Thias exclaimed with excitement. Not even acknowledging the fact that I had said goodbye.

"Yes I'll be here!"

"Yes!!!!!" Thias shouts with a fist pump. "See you later mama!!!"

I smiled as I watched him run into the school doors toward the cafeteria. We continue towards the stop sign. I only live 15 minutes from Thias's school, but I was still debating on whether or not I should let him take me all the way home. At this point, I think it's safe to say that I trust him. Ah, what the hell. I continued to give him directions to my apartment.

"So you are finally going to let me take you home, huh?" I laughed at him.

"Yes I believe I am. I think I can safely rule out you being a serial killer at this point."

We both laughed. "I'm glad I can make you laugh!"

"Yeah, you do. You actually have a pretty cool sense of humor."

"Ummm hmmm, I know. Turn right on the next street my apartment building is on the left." He makes the turn and pulls up in front of my apartment building. I began looking down at my hands, fiddling with my keys.

"So um, again I really appreciate you picking us up this morning. I am definitely tired."

"No problem, love. Gets some rest, I'll see you this afternoon, ok?" he assures me as he leans in kissing my forehead. Those lips, I would love to see what they feel like everywhere else.

"I'll be at work if you need me."

"Ok Arsen, thank you."

He watched me open my door before he pulled off. I watched him drive away before actually going inside. I threw my keys on the counter and headed to the shower. That water felt so good. I was feeling like Thias myself. I dried off and walked into my room with the towel around me. Putting my phone on the charger and placing it on the nightstand, I sat down on the bed and realized that no one was here but me. I didn't bother looking for clothes. I slid under the comforter and before I knew it my eyes grew heavy, until I could no longer fight it.

"Give me some more, more, more…..." The phone was ringing. I could vaguely hear that verse playing over and over. At first I thought I was dreaming. I just fell asleep it seemed. It couldn't possibly be time to go get Thias now. I hear the song again, this time much louder than the first as I was coming out of my slumber. I grabbed the phone snatching it off the nightstand. "Hello?"

"Hey love, how'd you sleep?"

"I don't know, I was still sleeping. What time is it?"

"It's 2 O'clock. I was on my way to come get you. Thias gets out of school at 2:45 right?" "Oh yeah he does. Ok I'm getting up now. Thanks for waking me up."

"It's ok. I'll be there in 20 minutes ok?"

"Sure, I'll be ready."

I jumped out of bed, grabbing my jeans and a tee shirt. Nothing too spectacular, since we'll be jumping around all evening. Thias is going to love this. After brushing my teeth and rinsing my face, I began to put on my clothes. There was a knock at the door. *"It seems like he is always on time."* I joked to myself. Walking down the hallway I attempt to put each sock on between strides. Opening the door, I see Arsen standing there with a Walmart bag.

"Come in, I just have to get my shoes and my jacket." He smiles walking past me, placing the bag on my dining room table. "What's that?" I asked.

"It's for Thias." he replied. I walk over to the table to be nosey. He lifts a box and turned it around for me to read it. It was a sleeping mat; one with way more cushion than the ones they sleep on at daycare. "Oh wow, you got this for him? I mean, thank you Arsen. You didn't have to do that. How much do I owe you?" I asked, hoping he wouldn't give me a price, being as though I had absolutely no money on me.

"Owe me?" he questioned. "Baby girl it's time to go, get your shoes!" he replied.

"But…." I began.

"But nothing. We don't need him standing outside waiting on us." I smiled and went to put my shoes on and grabbed my jacket. I appreciate him, I really do. I didn't have to ask. He just did it. He doesn't owe it to me to be this nice. I can't help but to feel like it's more to him. We headed out the door to the car. He, of course opened my door. By the time he had gotten in the car I remembered that I left my cellphone; but I didn't say anything. Everyone that I wanted to talk to would be with me anyway.

We continued on to Thias's school. I asked him about work and how he was feeling. He seemed a bit tired. I asked him questions about gifts he's received in the past; just to get an idea of what I should do for tomorrow. He was very vague. Almost as if he knew why I was asking and didn't want me to get anything. I have to do something really nice for him; he's so thoughtful and sweet. He deserves something amazing for Valentine's Day.

"You know I don't expect anything from you, right?" he asked.

"That doesn't mean you don't deserve it." I replied removing my seatbelt as we were pulling into the parking lot. Thias began skipping towards the car. I got out opening the door and strapping him in the seat belt.

"Hey mama! Hey Arsen!"

"What's going on little man? How was school?"

"Ahh, it was ok. We had a Valentine's Day party."

"Well that's nice Pumpkin" I replied. "Well Arsen has a surprise for you."

"COOL!!! What is it Arsen??" he was so excited.

"We will be there in about 30 minutes and you'll see."

"Aww man! I can't wait!!! I know it's going to be cool!!!"

We all laughed, Arsen turned the radio up as we made it to the highway. When we finally pulled up to SkyZone, Thias was ecstatic.

He was out of his seatbelt before we found a parking space. Arsen finally parked and we all headed inside. It was pretty packed to be 3:30 in the afternoon. Nonetheless, I was excited too; almost as excited as Thias. I haven't taken him on an outing in so long; I almost forgot what it was like to see him this excited. While Arsen is at the desk getting tickets, I began taking Thias's shoes off so he can get ready to jump around. Arsen walks back towards us.

"Sage, you want to go to the snack bar and get something to eat? I know he's probably hungry." he asked handing me a couple of twenty dollar bills.

"Ok, is there something you want?" He looks down at Thias. "What you want to eat little man?"

"Pizza!!!" Arsen looked back at me.

"Pizza." He replied. I smiled at both of them.

"Ok, I'll get Pizza." I headed towards the snack bar. No one was in line so I stood at the counter looking at the menu. "How can I help you?" the cashier asked as she was walking towards the counter. "I think I'll just get a large cheese pizza, with two medium drinks." Thinking Thias and I would just share a drink. He doesn't drink much soda anyway; neither do I. "You can make that a family meal and get a large bag of chips." she said pitching me on her sales techniques.

"Ok that sounds fine."

"That will be $27.76" I hand her both twenties. She rings it up and hands me the change. I stuffed it down in my pockets and turned to lean against the counter with my back facing her. I spotted Arsen and Thias running and jumping around the trampolines. Thias was laughing so hard he could barely jump. Every time Arsen caught up with him, he would throw him up in the air. Thias loved that. They looked like they were really father and son. My baby was so happy. He was really enjoying himself. I have to do something nice for Arsen tomorrow, he really deserves it.

"Ma'am....Ma'am?" I could hear the cashier trying to get my attention. I had been in a daze watching my son and my friend....my man. What? We are supposed to claim it right?

"Here are your cups, which bag of chips you want?" I looked over at the bags. I didn't know which kind Arsen would eat; probably, barbeque. All black people love barbecue, I know me and Thias do anyway. "Barbecue, is fine." She grabs the bag of chips and hands them to me. "Your pizza should be done in about 20 minutes." "Ok, thanks hun." I replied. I found an empty, clean table and sat our stuff down. I looked up to see Arsen and Thias running towards me with their shoes in their hand.

"Here you go mama!!!" Thias shouts handing me his shoes. Arsen places his under the table.

"You want to go jump with him love?" he asked.

"Oh nooooo! I'll just watch you guys! The pizza will be ready in 20 minutes." He leans over the table and kisses my forehead. Those lips!

"Ok, we will be back! Come on little man!!!"

"Ok Daddy!" Thias yelled with a smile on his face. I looked at Arsen to see if he was uncomfortable. He was smiling. I'm not asking him to play daddy, hell we not even together. What made Thias say that? We will definitely have to talk about this. They both take off running back towards the trampolines. I loved seeing the two interact with each other though. He's so good with him. I don't know where this is going or what this all means, but I really do hope it last forever. Tonight was great, tomorrow is going to be even better.

Chapter 6: Would You Be Mine?

"Happy Valentine's Day mama." Thias says as he walks into the bathroom holding a red heart shaped card." Awww! Thank you baby!" I sat down on the lid of the toilet to read it.

"Dear Mama, You are sooo beautiful and the sweetest mama I know, I luv you so very much. Happy Velentine's Day!" I looked at him and smiled. "Thank you baby! Did you see what mama got you?"

"Yep! Chocolate!!!! Can I take it to school Mama?"

As much as I wanted to say no, I decided to let him get away with it today because of this super sweet card he had just given me. "Just a few, not the whole bag ok?"

"Yay!! Thanks Mama!!"

"Ok hurry up so we can go to the bus stop!!" I slid on my sweatpants with the matching sweat shirt that had PINK written down the sides and my sneakers. Thias grabs his book bag and we head out the door. As I'm locking the door Thias runs down the stairs and instead of going toward the bus stop he turns to the left. I began walking down the steps calling his name. "Thias? Where are you....?" As soon as I reached the bottom of the steps, I notice Arsen parked to the left. Thias was already in the car. Arsen was standing at the passenger door waiting for me. I walked over to him and gave him a hug.

"You don't have to do this every day you know?" He kissed my forehead and leaned towards my ear. "As long as I'm breathing I will always make sure you and Thias are ok." I could literally feel his words running through my eardrums and stroking my heart strings like an echo, making my legs extremely weak. I leaned back looking him in his beautiful hazel eyes.

"I hope you never stop breathing." I whispered. He took his eyes off me for a second, as if he knew something I didn't. Taking my hand to guide me into the car he said,

"I will try my best not too." He closed the door and got in the car. "You ready Thias?" he asked.

"Sure am!!!" "Here you go mama." I looked back at Thias and he had flowers and three balloons, with one of the biggest white teddy bears I had ever seen in my life.

"Oh my goodness!!!!" I covered my mouth, I hadn't even noticed all of this when I got in the car. "This is for me??"

"Duh! Mama! Don't you like it?" I was speechless.

"Sage, do you like it?" Arsen asked. I looked over at him and without saying a word I threw my arms around his neck.

"I absolutely love it. You are amazing!" I spoke softly into his neck, trying to keep myself from crying. I could still feel a couple of teardrops fall down my cheek onto his neck. "Thank you so much!" I took the flowers from Thias as Arsen began to drive out the parking lot. I was overwhelmed it was all so beautiful.

"Have you found someone to watch Thias tonight?" he asked.

"Yeah, Shelly said she was going to watch him for me."

"Ok, well I have to work for a little while today. So I'll see you later on when it's time to pick Thias up from school." I nodded and continued to admire the flowers, smelling them and smiling to myself. When we pulled in front of the school, the administrator opened the back door for Thias. "See you guy's later." he said getting out the car. We both waved at him and watched him run into the school.

When we finally made it back to my apartment Arsen got out to help bring my gifts inside. "We will pick him up from school and I have to go back to work for a bit, but I'll be back around 7:30 to pick you up." he said.

"What should I wear? I mean should I dress up?" I asked.

"Don't worry too much about it. You'll be beautiful in whatever you put on."

I grabbed both sides of his face and kissed his lips. He kissed me back. As he headed towards the front door he tripped over one of my pumps. "Oh I'm sorry." I said slightly embarrassed. He picked it up and looked at it for a second, then slid it towards the side out of the walkway.

"It's ok. I'll be back. Call me if you need me."

"What if I just want to talk?"

"Call me if you just want to talk." he replied and walked out the door.

I put the flowers in a vase with some water and the teddy bear on my bed. I went to my room to finish painting the picture I had started for him last night when I got home. I had been painting for so long that I hadn't realized it was two o'clock already, until my phone began to ring.

"I'm on the way love." he said.

"Ok, I'm ready." I had paint all over my sweats and hands. Before long, my phone rang again.

"I'm outside."

"I'm coming out now." I replied. I slip my sneakers on and grabbed my keys, locking the front door. I walked down the steps and got into the car.

"Hey beautiful."

"Hey babe." I replied, covering my mouth in shock when I realized I called him babe. It just came out that way. He smiled.

"You got it right!"

We headed to the school to pick Thias up. Shelly had called me to let me know that she was going to pick Thias up early because her nephews were coming over too. Shelly and her girlfriend had broken up a while back. So instead of indulging in ice cream and romantic movies for Valentine's night, she decided to babysit for those who had dates. We made it back to the house, Thias and I rushed up the stairs to open the door, while Arsen was getting something out of his trunk. I left the front door cracked so he could just walk in.

"Baby, pack a little night bag. Shelly will be here in a while to get you. Her nephews are going to be with her."

"Mama you talking about Travis and Shaun?" he asked.

"Yes baby them two."

"YESSS!!!!" he shouted running to his room to pack a bag.

I laughed to myself; they are really going to drive Shelly crazy tonight. I walked down the hallway to see Arsen standing in the living room with two boxes. He looked at me and said "Don't open them until I leave, please?" I was a bit confused, but for some reason whenever he asked me to do something, I felt the need to listen. Kind of like a "Yes Daddy" moment. "I'll be back at 7:30."

"Ok I'll be ready." He kissed me and walked out the door.

As soon as the door closed I ran to the couch to open the boxes. The first box had something wrapped in red paper. There was a card on top with Shelly's name on it. Shelly? Confused, I open the card and out fell a $50 dollar bill with the words "Thank you for watching our son." *He really thought this through.* I thought to myself. I pulled opened the paper and lifted up a white long sleeved form fitting dress. I opened the other box and it had a red pair of platform pumps with an ankle strap; about 6 inches high. He has great taste. No wonder he didn't want me to worry about what I was going to wear; thinking back on when he tripped over one of my pumps. That's how he knew what size to get, huh? He thinks he's slick! I love it!!! He did and said everything right. He's almost too good to be true. I began cleaning up the house as Thias was watching cartoons on the couch. There was another knock at the door. This time it was Shelly and her nephews. She rushed in like the typical friend and headed straight towards my fridge.

"Girl, aint nothing in there!" I joked.

"You know I had to check." she said laughing, sitting down on the couch.

"Whose shoes are these?" she said picking up one of the red pumps. "And this dress???" I smiled.

"He bought that for me to wear tonight." I replied.

"Girl he got taste!!!" she exclaimed.

"Oh! I almost forgot." handing Shelly the card he had got her.

"What's this?"

"Stop asking so many questions and open it!!" We both laughed as she opened the card. The money fell out and she read the note. "Girl! He is definitely a keeper!!!"

"I know right?!" I looked over at the clock on the TV box. "It's 5:30, I gotta start getting ready."

"Ok, well we gonna go. Tell ya boo I said thank ya! And make sure you shave that twat! I know you got cobwebs!" she said laughing hysterically. "Boys!! Come on let's go!!" she yelled to the back. All three of them came stampeding down the hallway. I kneeled down next to Thias.

"You be good, ok? And listen!"

"Ok mama."

"Have fun girl! And be prepared to tell me all about it!"

"Ok love." I laughed. "And thanks!"

I went to my bathroom, turned on Pandora and jumped in the shower. I was definitely feeling myself. I took Shelly's advice, shaving everywhere that displayed unwanted hair. I then used my body scrub all over my body so I could feel extra soft. I haven't done this in a while. After I got out the shower and dried off, I began painting my toenails a rose red color; then my fingernails. I plopped down on my bed, landing on my back, for a few minutes to let my nails dry. I stared at the ceiling lost in my thoughts of what tonight had in store for me. I haven't had a companion worth having in a long time. Moments past and I realized that I am still completely naked and my nails are done drying. I look over at the clock on my night stand. It's already 6:30. He is typically on time so I should probably pick up the pace. I got up and began putting on makeup. I've never been good with makeup, so I just kept it simple as usual. A little filler for my eyebrows, eyeliner, mascara, and lipstick to match my nails. I was extremely excited, I felt like a little kid on the inside; jumping up and down, nervous all at the same time. I did sort of a basket weave with my locs from the back to the front, pinning them up into a bun that made a swoop over the right side of my forehead. *"Maybe that would make him kiss my lips instead of my forehead tonight."* I joked to myself.

I lotioned my entire body before slipping into a black bra and thong set. I didn't want any lines to show through the dress, although I find thongs to be very uncomfortable. I slide into the dress, it fits perfectly. The bottom was pencil and it reached right to the middle of my knees; not too short and not too long. The dress fit my curves and gave me just enough space around my midsection to where I couldn't notice my stomach. I felt extremely sexy looking in the bathroom mirror. I put on my round, gold earrings that covered the bottom of my ear. I figured I'd keep it sophisticated and not wear anything dangling with my bun. I picked up a gold charm bracelet Thias and Shelly gave me for my birthday last year. I stepped back to admire myself a little bit. I walked in my room to gather Arsen's painting, putting it in the living room so he could see it when he walked in. I run back to the bathroom as I forgot to put on some perfume. Just as I began to spray a couple sprays, I hear a knock at the door. I peek out the bathroom looking at the clock. Damn! He is always on time. I sit down on the bed to strap on the red pumps. He knocks again, and I trip my way down the hallway trying to buckle the last strap. I get to the door standing up straight and adjusting my dress, trying to look perfect. I began smiling from ear to ear as I open the door, there stood Arsen. He had on a long sleeve white button down Polo shirt, with dark jeans, and a blazer. He looked like he had just stepped out of the GQ magazine. Fresh haircut, face shining, shirt pressed to the tee. *"Look at my man."* I thought; just look at him.

"You look absolutely beautiful, love." he said.

"Thanks! You look amazing yourself. Come in for a second, I have something to show you." I demanded politely. He steps in and I point towards the painting. "Now you can't take it with you tonight, because it still needs to dry a little." He began staring at the painting. He wasn't saying anything, I began to get nervous. "Do you like it?" I asked. He continued to stare before looking at me replying.

"I love it. It's me and you, but why are you crying?" he asked. The painting showed the wind blowing my locs in my face as tears flowed from one eye peeking through my locs. In the background I painted him with a crown on his head walking towards me.

"They're tears of joy." I explained. "This painting depicts my King finding me and healing my broken heart." He looked at me as if he were accepting the honor. "We should probably go." I continued.

"Yes, we should be there by 8:15." We headed out to the car as he helped me down the stairs.

"I'd sure hate to bust my tail before we get to where we going." I laughed to myself.

As we were getting into the car he turned to me and said, "Baby girl, it's just me and you." I smiled, sitting back in my seat gazing out the window.

"Yes it is." I replied.

We made it to the restaurant. It was amazing, so many couples. We were completely surrounded by laughter and love. We quickly joined in as we sat at our table and placed our orders. The entire time we never took our eyes off each other. We occasionally held each other's hands, laughing and talking hours away. Our smiles matched the chemistry. If the perfect world never existed before in my life, it did tonight. Arsen grabbed my hand as we were leaving out the restaurant, making our way back into the car. He held it the entire walk, never letting go. As we head home, I began thanking him for such an amazing night. Of course he was so modest and humble. As we pulled in the parking lot of my apartment, he told me that he would walk me to the door. In my mind I was hoping he did a little more than that, but I agreed. As I opened the door I stood there wishing he would follow me in.

He stood at the steps not even crossing the threshold. I kind of got the hint at that point. "Good night beautiful and thank you for tonight." I smiled.

"I'm the one that should be thanking you. This whole day was amazing; but goodnight." I replied squeezing the door knob trying to fight the urge of wanting to pull him inside. "Goodnight love." he said staring into my eyes. I began to slowly close the door when he stopped it with his hand. I opened it back up. He looks at me and says, "I didn't get the chance to ask you, but would you be mine?"

My heart dropped, but I tried to keep it together as to not look weak. "You mean your Valentine?" I replied sarcastically.

He stepped over the threshold and grabbed me around my waist. "No, would you be my woman?" he said. Before I could even respond our lips touched. He gripped one hand tighter around my waist and the other he cuffed the back of my neck. Kissing me deeper and making me weaker. He began to walk my body backwards, pushing me up against the wall; caressing my neck with his tongue. He began to tease me, biting my bottom lip. My breathing becomes heavy, and my vision blurry as the throbbing sensation between my legs grew more intense with every kiss. My knees weaken as he glides one hand down the side of my thigh, pulling my dress up to my waist. I reached for the collar of his blazer, pulling it down over his shoulders, gripping his head as he nibbled on my neck. He slid one arm out of the blazer, allowing it to hang from his arm that was still gripping my waist; before turning me around to face the wall. I rest my face against the wall, clutching my bottom lip with my teeth; with both hands up as if I was being frisked by the police. I could feel his body pressing against mine, as the print of his hard penis rest against me. He began to grab the strings of my thongs sliding them down below my butt. My eyes still closed, anticipating each moment, I could feel him sliding down to his knees. He began to kiss my hips and ass, alternating between bites and kisses as both his hands grip and massage each cheek. I inhale as I feel the wetness of the tip of his tongue slide down the crack of my ass. As he began to savor the taste of me, I start to moan. My head began to get light and the chills rushed through every inch of me. Suddenly we hear my neighbor's door opening, as I forgot to close the front door behind him. He pulls my dress down to my knees, turning me around and hugging me. She walks out and waves. I waved back. We both looked at each other and laughed at the fact that neither of us realized the door was opened. Nor did we

know what all she seen. We could hear her
going down the steps.

He kisses my neck and then my lips, before
saying, "Goodnight Love." My body
screaming at him Noooooo!!! Don't you
dare leave me like this! I closed my eyes and
smiled replying, "Yes."

"Yes what?"

"Yes I will be yours." I said. He smiled,
holding both sides of my face kissing my
forehead, nose, and then my lips.

"Thank you, that's all I needed to hear
tonight." he said, before walking out and
closing the door behind him. I let out a deep
breath, walking into my bathroom. As I ran
a cold shower, I couldn't help but smile.
Even though I didn't get "none", this was
still the best Valentine's Day.

Chapter 7: From This Day Forward

The sun snuck its way through my bedroom window, the rays hitting my eyelids. I could even hear birds chirping rather rapidly. That's a first, or maybe this could be the first time I actually paid attention. Waking up this morning was quite different than most lately. A feeling of peace came over me. My mental vision was clearer and my hearing more intense. I find it hard to believe that a person could enhance my soul this way; but then again, isn't that what we are here for....to elevate our souls through this journey? I opened my eyes, glancing around the room. The sun broke through every possible crack, as if an angel was descending down from the Heavens straight into my room. My phone rang, startling me. I reached to answer it and then it stopped. I picked it up anyway to see who was calling. Shelly. As I was getting ready to redial her number she called back.

"Hey girl! What's up? You boo'ed up?" I rubbed my hand across my face then dropped it onto the bed, in disappointment.

"No chick. I'm solo this morning."

"Whaat?? What happened? Or what didn't happen I should say?" she continued.

"Oh girl, it was about to happen! We were interrupted by the girl next door!" I replied laughing. "I'll tell you about it later, when I feel like taking another cold shower. How'd my baby do last night? Was he good?"

"Yes hunny, he was an angel. It's my nephews that got on my damn nerves! Thias is so sweet though. He was asking about you all night."

"I know child! He is not used to being without me."

"Well, he is a little mama's boy. But I was just calling to see if I can keep him one more day?"

"Girl no! I miss my baby!"

"Look, you gotta learn to let him spread his wings Sage! I'm going to take care of him. I promise. I'm taking my nephews to Six Flags today and Thias is already sold on the idea. Please?"

"What am I going to do today Shelly?"

"I don't know heffa! Try being a woman!" she laughed. "Go out with ya man! You the only mama I know that has objections about someone volunteering to keep their child. You a mess!"

"Ok well just let me talk to him for a second." She began calling Thias's name for him to come to the phone.

"Hey mama! We going to Six Flags today!!"
I could feel his smile through the phone.
"Ok baby. Mama misses you."
"Moooom!" he whined. "I only been gone
one night. What would you do without me?"
"I'd really be lost, baby." I responded.
"Make sure you wear your long sleeve shirt
today. It's pretty out, but it's still supposed
to be a little windy."
"Ok mama, I love you. See you later!"
Before I could say I love you too he had
already handed Shelly back the phone.
"See girl! He aiight! Now go get you a life!"
We both laughed.
"Well do you need some money for the
tickets? I got a few dollars."
"Naw, we good. My sister gave me three
free kids' passes yesterday."
"Ok. I appreciate you girl."
"No problem love, see you later." I hung up
the phone and sat up on the side of the bed. I
have no idea what to do with myself right
now. My phone rang again, this time it was
Silk.
"Good morning love." he answered. "How
did you sleep last night?"
"I slept pretty good, but I woke up feeling
amazing."
"Has Thias made it back yet?"
"You won't believe this! I just got off the
phone with Shelly and she asked to keep

him another day. They are going to Six Flags." He began to laugh.

"What's so funny?" I asked.

"The fact that you literally sound hurt that he's not coming home today."

"Oh yeah? That's same thing Shelly said. He's my life."

"Yes he is, but you have to find yourself somewhere in there too. Have you had breakfast yet?"

"Not yet, I'm literally just getting up."

"Well, let me come cook our first breakfast as a couple." I could tell he was smiling.

"Ok, King. Hurry up! I miss you."

We hung up the phone and I began to tidy up and bathe before his arrival. I wasn't two seconds out the tub before I heard a knock at the door. Leaving out the bathroom, I grabbed my robe and wrapped it around me as I was headed down the hallway towards the front door. I didn't bother to check the peephole, I knew who it was.

"Good morning beautiful." he said standing there with two grocery bags in each hand. This man even went grocery shopping. I mean, my fridge is far from full but I had enough for a little breakfast. I watched him place the bags on the kitchen counter as I was sure to close and lock the front door this time. I walked over hugging him from behind as he was putting away the groceries.

"I was just getting out the shower when you got here." I said backing up towards the kitchen table.

"You want to wait until I get dressed to start cooking? So I can show you where everything is at?"

Without saying a word he began walking towards me. He raised his hand running his finger down the side of my face. He went down to my shoulder, then over my breast; leaving a trail of weakness in my body as he got closer to the belt of my robe that was keeping me covered. With one finger he pulled my belt loose, the sides open up displaying every inch of my curves. I allowed the robe to slide off my shoulders and down my arms; watching him as he admires me, while biting on his bottom lip. The robe hits the floor; he cuffs one arm under my ass while the other hand is under my arm lifting me onto the table. Leaning over me he slides my decorative center piece down the table as it just barely hangs on to the edge. He grabs the back of my neck, placing another hand on my shoulder, gently laying me back on the table. I looked down, watching him pull up a chair and sit down in front of me; as if his breakfast had been served. He places his hands under my knees pushing them back into a butterfly. I began taking in deep breathes as I can tell where this was going. He scoots his chair up closer and places one finger inside me. I gasped for air as if this was my first time. He began to kiss on my clit, pecking her with his lips so as to tease her at first. As he moved his finger in and out….in and out, he began twirling his tongue in a figure eight motion around her, occasionally sucking her into his mouth. I gripped both sides of the table trying to keep my composure, but it was too much. My legs were shaking and with every stroke of his finger, my moans elevated to a higher pitch. I began to soak his finger, which encouraged him to go faster. He watched my face to make sure he was pleasing me right. I could feel the chills running to my head. I couldn't close my mouth and my vision was turning into dots and swirls of light. Like, I was literally coming out of my body. He began to speed up his strokes this time going deeper. I could feel myself about to explode. He hit the perfect spot, and by reflex I grabbed that back of his head to ensure he wouldn't leave that spot.

"Baby, please don't stop. I'm there." I begged him. I began thrusting my hips as if I was riding his face. My pussy throbbing, I began to shout telling him I can't take anymore; as I reached my end he kept going. He didn't come up for air. My legs were shaking uncontrollably. I placed both feet on his shoulder pushing him back, sliding myself on the table. He leaned back in the chair and smiled. It felt so good I was embarrassed. He picked me up wrapping my legs around his waist carrying me into my room. Kissing me, allowing me a taste of his breakfast, He laid me on the bed. I watched as he began to undress. First his shoes, his shirt, pants, and then boxers. I smiled. He was a little man but the package was oversized. He climbed over me, resting his body on mine. Looking me in my eyes and pushing my locs out of my face, he asked, "You sure?" I reached down wrapping my hand around the shaft of his dick guiding it into my already throbbing pussy. "I'm sure." I replied. He began kissing my neck as he slid inside me. It's been a minute, but the pain felt so good. He moans, his face full of pleasure. We had gotten lost inside the moment, inside each other. I held onto his strong arms as our bodies connect. He was everything. He was perfect in every way. I began to tighten around his dick as I was about to explode. He couldn't hold it any longer. He gripped my locs with one hand and my thigh with the other as he thrust deeper inside me. In the same moment we both let go. My legs still shaking, he laid there inside me. The only movement was the rise and fall of our chest. *That was amazing.* I thought to myself. He finally lay beside me, bringing my body close to his.

"I don't ever want to go a day without seeing you from this day forward….the rest of my life." he said.

"Awww baby, that's just the sex talk!" I said jokingly. "One day I'm going to get on your nerves and you're gonna ignore me the whole day." I laughed.

He placed one finger under my chin lifting my head so our eyes connect. "I'm going to spend the rest of my life with your little aggravating tail." he smiled. "You hungry now? You distracted me from cooking!"

"Me? Oh no! You will not put this on me!" We both laughed as he pulled me in even closer. "Are you hungry?" I asked.

"Not really, but I was going to cook for you."

"I'm not hungry right now. Can we just lay here for a minute? Can you just hold me? I feel safe in your arms."

"Baby girl as long as I'm breathing, you and Thias will always be safe."

I wrapped my leg around him, snuggling my face closer to hear his heartbeat. Closing my eyes listening to the thump of his chest, I prayed his heart would never stop beating. Suddenly, I found myself fast asleep in my Kings arms.

Chapter 8: Love Spell

As the days went on, Arsen kept his promise. He made sure that we saw each other every single day. Work for him was starting to pick up with the rainy season, so to keep the fire in our love life; I'd pop up on him for an occasional quickie. At first he was shy, like the only place he could make love to me was in a bed; but after a few rounds in the work truck, he loosened up. Our relationship was blossoming into something amazing. I could trust him with my life, my child, my heart; everything. I was finally able to leave the night shift gig and do more painting, as Arsen began to help me out financially so that I could pursue my dreams. I thanked God I had someone like him in my and Thias's life. I never imagined I could be this happy.

"Mama! Am I going to Auntie Shelly house tonight?" Thias asked, as if he didn't already know from eavesdropping on my phone conversation.

"Yes, Hunnie, you are. Me and Arsen are going out tonight for a while." I replied.

"Mama?" He looks at me with the puppy dog eyes, like he knew he was about to ask a question I could possibly say no to.

"Can I call Arsen Daddy?" he asked.

For a moment I was stunned. Arsen is the first man that has been around him since I left his father. I didn't really know how to answer that.

"How about this Pumpkin, I'll let you have that conversation with Arsen, ok?" He smiled, sliding out my room in his socks. I definitely have to prepare Arsen for this conversation. Someone began knocking at the door. "Thias!" I yelled from the bathroom door. "Go see who that is!" I could hear him running down the hallway bumping into the walls. The door opens then it close.

"Girrrllll!!!" I could hear Shelly coming down the hallway, getting closer to my room. "Girl! I got some tea for ya ass, hunnie!!!" she said, ready to gossip as she sat down on my bed.

"Oh lawd! What's up?" I asked not really wanting to know, but being polite.

"Guess who's pregnant?"

"Who, child?"

"Tanya!" I began to laugh. I thought she was really going to tell me something worth hearing. "You act like that is a big surprise. I thought you were going to tell me you were pregnant!" I shook my head walking back into the bathroom.

"Chile! That is not the tea baby!!!" she exclaimed even more excited to spill the second half of the news. "Guess who she pregnant by?"

I came back to the bathroom door looking at her with the lipstick in my hand. "You gonna tell me or do you really want me to try to guess out of all the dudes that done put miles on her?" I replied sarcastically.

"Shaun Girl!" she said laughing leaning backwards on the bed.

"Shaun!! You are lying!!!" I began to laugh with her. I always thought Shaun was a little fruity in the booty. I guess my gay-dar is out of whack. "I cannot believe he went up in her raw!" She looked at me with tears in her eyes from all the laughing she was doing.

"Believe it baby!! Because it happened!! And he excited and telling everybody too girl! She's all embarrassed, talking about she wants to get an abortion and stuff. This is like the funniest work soap opera shit I've ever experienced!"

Shelly always had the scoop on everybody and everything. People loved talking to her, telling all their business like she was a counselor or something. "Anyway child! That was my laugh for today. What you and Mr. Man doing tonight?"

"I don't know girl, he said he had somewhere special he wanted to take me."

"I can't wait until I find me a woman like Arsen." I began to coughing as if I had choked on my spit.

"Well hunnie you won't find a woman like Arsen baby. He don't have feminine tendencies." I replied jokingly.

"You know what I meant heffa!" she said stomping out of my room. "Thias! You ready to go baby? My nephew will be on the way soon." There was another knock on the door.

"Shelly get that please, it's Arsen."

Shelly walked down the hallway to get the door. I could hear mild chatter from the two as they greeted each other.

"See you later mama!" Thias yelled in my room on his way down the hallway to speak to Arsen.

I could hear all three of them conversing with each other. I slid on my sandals to match my sundress. The weather was supposed to be nice tonight. Cool spring air with a slight chance of rain; but that's April weather for you. I walked down the hallway.

"Alright girl, we out!" Shelly said as she was picking up Thias's night bag.

"Ok love, see y'all later." I replied giving Thias a kiss, as he was in such a rush to leave out the door. He enjoys spending time with Shelly's nephews. He's so used to me keeping him in the house; he rarely gets to play with kids his age. They walked out the door and Arsen greets me with a kiss.

"You know what Thias asked me?" he said. I already had a pretty good idea, but dreading the answer he gave Thias, I pretended that I didn't.

"No, what's that babe?"

"He asked if he could call me Daddy." he said with a smile on his face.

"Oh?" I replied. "What did you say?"

"I told him if that is how he felt, and then yes he could." I let out a huge sigh of relief. "I am fonder of Thias, and then he is of me." I smiled.

"Well he admires you a lot Arsen. You are the only male figure in his life."

"You ready to go? I figured we'd go out to eat and take a walk downtown tonight."

"I'm glad I decided to wear flats." I laughed. We stopped at a few restaurants downtown. It seemed like everywhere we went there was over an hour wait. We finally decided to just get some take out and go to the park and eat. As we enjoyed our meal and each other's company, I couldn't help but notice the man sitting on the bench across from us. He was very tall and dark skinned, dressed in all black. He wasn't thuggish, but very well put together. He wasn't doing anything, just sitting there flipping through his tablet. I had seen that same man earlier in the evening at a few other restaurants that we were at tonight. It couldn't have been a coincidence; it was almost as if he were following us. I leaned over placing my head on Arsen shoulder as to not be obvious. "Baby, that man has been following us all night. I'm starting to feel a little uncomfortable." I complained.

"Don't worry about it love, I got you." he said. I couldn't help but notice that he didn't ask me who I was talking about, like he already knew. "Let's get up and take a little walk." he suggested.

We began to walk and after a few minutes of not seeing the strange man anymore I began to relax. It was so beautiful outside. It was the perfect cool breeze air. We walked down the sidewalks moving through the hustle and bustle of Atlanta's nightlife. People were hanging outside of bars; some drunk, others well on their way. We walked past a few vacant storefronts; but it was one that really caught my eye. I stopped to admire the wide display window, cuffing my hands to peek into the dark store space. I couldn't see anything. I could feel Arsen standing close behind me.

"What are you thinking?" he asked. I stepped back from the store window just to stare at the entire front.

"This would be a perfect spot for my gallery." I said, still staring hopelessly through the store window.

"You will have your gallery soon, Baby. I'm making sure of it." he assured me.

He grabbed my hand tugging me away from the window so that we could continue walking. I looked back at the store front to get one last look before we left, when I noticed the man in black following close behind us. I turned around as subtle as possible.

"Baby!" I whispered to Arsen. "That guy, he is still following us. What does he want?"

"I know love, don't worry I got you." he said.

He never answered my question. He just began picking up the pace holding onto my arm as we weaved through the crowd. I was completely confused. He wasn't saying anything, he never looked back. Who was this guy? Why was he following us? Arsen pulled me down an alley between two warehouses. I snatched away from him.

"What is going on damnit?" I demanded. Without saying a word he grabbed my arm again and pushing me up against a dumpster, making me slide down to the ground. He put his finger against my lips as if to tell me to be quiet. I could hear footsteps coming down the alley way. Arsen stood up and walked from behind the dumpster.

"You are hard man to get a hold of Ace." I could hear a man's voice. "I would say we need to talk but we are sort of past that point now." he continued. I was kneeling on the ground trying not to make a sound. Arsen was still in my eye sight. He stood there with his hands crossed in front of him. "You're right. We are past that now." he said to the mystery man.

In that moment Arsen charged at the man. I could hear them wrestling, punches being thrown. I tried not to peek but then there was a noise, almost like a whistle blew; with a flash of light. I stood up over the dumpster scared that it was Arsen who had been shot. I could see the two still struggling. Arsen hits the man and the gun flew towards me, sliding in front of the dumpster. They both continued to punch each other. I could hardly see, but the man was so much taller and bigger than Arsen. Somehow, they ended up on the ground and the man was on top of Arsen punching him repeatedly. I grabbed the gun. I had never shot a gun before but I pointed it trying to aim it just right. I closed my eyes and pulled the trigger. I heard the sound of the whistle. This gun had a silencer. All of a sudden the commotion stopped. I opened my eyes and saw a lumpy figure lay on the ground. I ran over thinking I had shot Arsen. The body began to move. I could barely see Arsen's face. He began pushing the dead man off of him. My hands began to shake and I started crying. Arsen rolled the body over, and a piece of gold medal fell out of the man's pocket. I bent down to pick it up. It was a police badge.

"Oh my goodness, I'm going to jail! I just killed a police officer." I began crying.

I still had the gun in my hand, which was shaking uncontrollably. I couldn't believe what I'd just done. I couldn't live with myself. Arsen stood up and slowly reached for the gun. Taking it out of my hand, he began wiping it down with his shirt; as if he was getting rid of my fingerprints. I looked at him, with anger in my eyes. He stuffed the gun down in his pants and took his bloody button down shirt off, leaving on his wife beater. Something about this was all too familiar for him; like he had done this before. Still not saying anything he grabbed the man by his legs and began to lift him into the dumpster. I was still standing there in shock, confused and scared. *"I thought I knew him."* I thought to myself. He walked back towards me and grabbed my arm. I snatched away from him once more.

"I just threw my whole life away and I have no idea why." I manage to spit out through my tears. He began to wipe the tears from my eyes.

"You saved my life." he said.

"Who was he? Why was he following us Arsen?"

"Come on Sage." he said grabbing my hand once more.

"No!" I yelled at him.

"You tell me what I just did… And why? I bought you around my son. Who are you Arsen?"

"Listen, I am everything that you think I am. I can't explain anything to you right now. We have to get out of here. I love you Sage. I'll never hurt you. If you don't believe anything else you have to believe that. Please baby, let's go. I'll answer whatever questions you may have once we are home."

I looked at him. I fell victim to his love spell once again. I wanted an explanation, but I was too weak at that moment to demand one. Even after tonight's strange events, I trusted him. I believed everything he said to me. He reached for my hand once more, and I gave it to him. He grabbed my hand, and after a few left and right turns we ended back up on a major street. We walked back in the direction in which we had come, passing the storefront I was admiring moments earlier. I looked at it again, thinking that I would never get the chance to open that gallery now. I just took the life of a cop. We finally made it back to the park where we had left the car earlier. He opens the passenger door for me to sit down. Still a little stiff I managed to gather myself to get in the car. He stopped at the trunk to retrieve a bag before getting in the front seat. The whole ride back to my house was silent. I didn't say anything to him. I couldn't even look at him. I never would have thought that I would be in a situation like this because of him. Tears continued to flow from my eyes as my mind was in frenzy. A whirlwind of thoughts consumed me. *"Who would take care of my son if I had to go to prison? How did I get to this point in my life? Dick! Good damn, hypnotizing DICK!"* That is the only logical explanation. I knew he was too good to be true. His real name probably isn't even Arsen. It's probably Deshawn, and he might be a wanted bank robber or something. Why else would an undercover cop follow him around all night? I was so furious on the inside; but I loved him too. I don't know if he realized that was the first time he told me he loved me. Hell if he saved my life, I'd probably tell him I love him too. Too bad he just ruined mines, and for some reason I still loved him. We pulled up to my apartment, and I quickly jumped out the car heading towards my door. I could hear him following close behind. I opened the door and he followed me in. I threw my keys and purse on the counter and ran to the bathroom and turned on the shower; hoping that it would wash away the sins I have committed tonight. I began to undress, stepping into the shower; scrubbing my entire body as if I had just come in contact with a horrible disease. I began to cry. My heart was in such turmoil, I couldn't think. I could hear Asren enter the bathroom and through the curtain I could see him sit on the toilet.

"Sage, I'm not going to let anything happen to you. I'm getting rid of the gun." he started.

I continued to ignore him as he was still not saying what I needed to hear. "Seven years ago." he began. "I killed a man."

I stopped scrubbing, my heart sank. Isn't this something you tell someone on the first date? Like, Hi my name is Arsen, I like to go to the movies and read. I have amazing pipe game and I've also killed someone. No worries though, that was years ago.

"He raped and killed my pregnant wife because I owed him a lot of money. I shot him three times in the head, in front of his brother who had him in handcuffs walking him into the courthouse. That man tonight, was his brother."

I pulled the shower curtain back, to look at him; water still running down my body.

"I pled temporary insanity and did five years for involuntary manslaughter. His brother wanted me dead, ever since I got out of prison."

I stepped out the shower, wrapping my arms around his neck. My heart began to bleed for him. I always knew it was something sad in his eyes.

"Why didn't you tell me?" I asked.

"I didn't want you to not be with Me." he said. "It's a part of my past that I don't want to remember."

"Baby but it's a part of you. It makes you who you are. I love you Arsen. There is nothing you can't tell me baby." I assured him. "What am I supposed to do now?" I asked him. "I just took a man's life trying to protect you, protect us. What about my son?"

He pulled my naked wet body close to him, resting his head onto my stomach.

"I don't want you to worry about anything. I will take care of it all. You'll never hear about any of this again." he said. Then looking up at me with those beautiful, sad hazel eyes he said, "I don't want to lose you Sage, just promise me you'll stay."

I began to soothe the back of his head with both my hands. I couldn't leave him; not after all he's been through. Tonight wasn't his fault. It wasn't either of our faults. It's just something that happened, and we couldn't control. I just pray that God and the Universe understand. I'm no killer. I was just trying to protect the ones I love. He is my man. I have to stand by him no matter what. I continue to caress his head.

"I love you baby, I'm not going anywhere. You just have to trust me enough to tell me the truth. No more secrets, ok? I put my life on the line. You take care of this and we never have to mention it ever again." He wrapped his arms around my waist, holding me tight. "I love you Sage." The words that made me weak….the love spell.

Chapter 9: Part Of The Family

Given the circumstances, I understood Arsen and why he did what he did many years ago. I would have possibly done the same thing. The next couple of months were really rough for me though. I couldn't get over what I had done; and my conscious was extremely heavy. Regardless, of whether it was self-defense or not, that man had a life; A family. How could I ever forgive myself, continue on with my life as if nothing ever happened? I prayed constantly asking God to forgive me; asking him to understand. I laid in the bed staring at the ceiling, barely in my right mind. I know he sensed that something was bothering me. He rolled over, pulling me close to him. I could feel the heat from his body, sending chills down my spine. He leans in closer to my ear. "Sage, you're my angel. You saved my life." he said trying to comfort my guilty conscious. He eased his hand down the side of my thigh under the cover. Softly kissing my bottom lip, I could feel him sliding my panties to the side. He began gently rubbing my clit in a circular motion. I inhaled deeply as my head began to feel light and there was a tingle in my nipples. I opened my legs to make it easier for him; letting out a slight moan, so to encourage him. Then there was a knock on my bedroom door. Arsen turned over lying on his back as I sat up in the bed, leaning against the headboard. The first time ever Thias knocks on any doors. I was quite surprised.

"Daddy?" he says as he pushes the door open slowly. He sticks his head in and once he noticed that Arsen and I are up looking towards the door he barges in, jumping on the bed. "We are going to meet my grandma today?" he asked Arsen. "Yep little man! Your uncles too." Arsen replied. Arsen had invited us over to his mother's house for Sunday dinner today. That is the part of all this I love the most. How much Thias loves him and looks forward to being a part of his family. All of that feels so good, except what happened a few nights ago. I can't get that out of my head. All I could think about was watching the news and seeing how they were looking for this cop. For the life of me I find it hard to believe that his body hasn't been found yet. I mean, I watch a lot of CSI and Law and Order. How hard is it to find a body in the dumpster? I know he tried to kill us, but his family at least deserves closure. I have to stop thinking about this, but I don't know how. "Thias go get one of your nice outfits to wear and get ready for a bath." He looked at me with his lips poked out, like he was all for everything else except the bath part. He jumped off my bed and ran to his room. I could see Arsen staring at me out the corner of my eye. He reached behind me rubbing my back. "Sage, don't think too much about it. Try to enjoy today please." he said. I looked over at him and shook my head getting up to get in the shower. As I stepped out the shower to get dressed, Arsen came in the bathroom. I'm standing there naked in the mirror as I always do, staring and criticizing my imperfect body. He stands behind me as if he knows what I am thinking. I stare at him through the mirror as he pulls his shorts down. My body still wet from the shower, he began to caress my back in an upward motion before finally reaching my shoulders and pushing me forward. I lean over the sink as my locs hang in my face, I watch him; our eyes connecting through the mirror. I feel him sliding the tip of his dick between my ass. I lift up on the tip of my toes, slightly arching my back so he can enter. I gasp for air as I feel him inside me, both hands on either side of my hips. He holds on tight, as he pushes deeper with every stroke. I raise my right leg resting my knee on the edge of the sink. He moans, gripping me tighter as he was able to go even deeper in this position; the entire time biting his bottom lip and admiring the plumpness of my heart shaped ass. I leveraged my leg on the sink and began bouncing back on his dick, encouraging him to go faster. The sound of my ass hitting his stomach with every push began to get louder and more intense. He made me weak. I began to tighten around him, reaching my arm backwards to push him. He kept stroking and I began to climax. He could feel me. He grabbed both of my shoulders and began to push deeper and deeper. Letting out a deep breath, he stopped. He leaned over, still inside me, kissing my back. Finally he turned around to run a shower. I stayed there for a second unable to lift my leg from the sink. Turning around, I watched him lather his body with soap. I admired him, he was everything. There was a knock on the bathroom door; I jumped as it startled me. I reached for the towel and wrapped it around me to open the door.

"How do I look Mama?" Thias said standing there with both arms out so that I could get the best view of his outfit. He had on Polo. A Polo navy blue shirt, with a sort of burnt orange pair of shorts with a navy blue Polo symbol at the bottom, and matching Polo shoes. I stood back to look at him. I don't remember this outfit at all and I am almost absolutely positive I didn't buy it. I'm not a fan of name brand clothing. It's all overrated to me.

"Pumpkin you looking real clean." I said. "But I didn't buy that outfit." He looked at me smiling.

"I know Mama, Daddy did." he replied. I turned back looking toward the shower to get confirmation from Arsen. Arsen shrugged his shoulders and turned around to finish rinsing off. Thias had turned around to head back to his room and I closed the bathroom door, stepping back into the shower to freshen up.

"You don't have to buy him all those name brand clothing, Arsen." I began. "You do enough already. I mean I don't expect you to pay all the bills and buy clothes too, you know? "He had a silent way of hushing me with his eyes. He leaned over pecking my lips before getting out of the shower.

"You don't expect anything, Sage." he said, drying off with the towel. "That is why I'm going to give you the world."

I held onto the shower curtain watching him as he wrapped the towel around him and walked out the bathroom. I freshened up in the shower and stepped out. Putting on a little make up and tying my dreads back, I walked out the bathroom; only to find the two most important men sitting on my bed, dressed just alike in the same Polo outfit. It was the most adorable thing I had seen in a while and in that moment I forgot about everything that was bad.

"Well, I guess we all gonna be matching today, huh?" I said pulling a navy blue sundress out of my closet.

"Come on Little man! Let's let your mama get dressed. You know women always the last to get ready." he joked, as he lifts Thias off the bed and carried him into the living room.

I continued to get dressed, spraying on a little perfume. Gathering my purse and phone I walked down the hallway. Those two were sitting on the couch watching cartoons. "I'm ready you two!" I said smiling. Thias looked up jumping off the couch. Arsen got up, turned off the TV, and we all walked out the house and to the car.

Arsen's mother lived in Roswell, about thirty minutes from my house. The whole ride there Arsen and Thias were giving each other math problems to solve off the top of their head. I, on the other hand, was extremely nervous; wondering if his mother and brothers would like me. *"Hell even if they didn't, it's too late now."* I thought to myself. He's stuck with me. Finally we pulled up to a nice, four sided brick house with a two car garage. There were two other cars there, both flashy with matching rims like Arsen's. We all got out the car and walked up the sidewalk as Arsen opened the door. My stomach was still full of butterflies. I could hear some men talking as we entered the house. Arsen had Thias's hand as we made our way down the hall to the kitchen. Arsen turned the corner, and an elderly woman let out a high pitch scream of excitement.

"My baby!!!" she said grabbing Arsen by both ears, kissing him repeatedly in his face. His face was still a little sore from the altercation the other night. I could tell it was hurting him as she pinched and pulled his face. "What happened to you Ace?" she asked. "You're not in any trouble are ya?" "No mama! Just had a little run in that's all." he responded.

She stepped back and crossed her arms. She was a sweet looking old lady; very stout and round. Her hair was gray and she had one French braid going towards the back that hung past her shoulders, she looked almost as if she was a full blooded Indian. I look over to the table. There were two men, both significantly taller and buffer than Arsen. They each looked like they had done ten years pumping nothing but iron.

"Well aren't you going to introduce us?" she said analyzing me and Thias from a distance.

"Mama, this is my son Thias and my......" he paused as if he had to think of my title. "My fiancé, Sage." He looked back at me and began, "Sage this is my mother, Lillian; and my brothers Jerod and Malachi." They both stood up to greet me and Thias. Still a bit nervous I reached out to give his mother a hug, fearing rejection.

"It's nice to finally meet you all. It's my pleasure." I said, trying to be as polite as possible. His mother gave me a hug.

"Yes it's nice to finally meet this mystery woman that stole my Ace's heart…" she paused. "So quickly, I might add." she said in a bit of a sarcastic tone.

His brothers walked toward me reaching for my hand. Each planted a kiss on either hand, and then acknowledged Thias with a high five. His mother walked back into the kitchen and began cooking. A little girl ran down the stairs calling one of the men her dad. "Thias this is Serenity, my niece. Why don't y'all go outside and play?" Arsen told him.

"Ok Daddy!" Serenity took Arsen by the hand and they both ran out the back door to play.

Arsen sat down at the table and began talking with his brothers. I walked into the kitchen to see if his mother wanted my help. She was hesitant at first.

"Wash your hands and cut up some lettuce for the salad." she demanded. I politely did as I was told. "So what do you do for a living Sage?" she asked.

"I'm an artist." I replied proudly. "I hope to open up a gallery someday. "She paused from stirring the spaghetti noodles in the pot.

"Where are your parents?" she asked.

Older people tend to ask a lot of questions. It didn't bother me though. I wasn't ashamed of my truth. "I don't really know mam." I replied, focusing on the knife and the lettuce. "I grew up in foster care."

"Hmm…." she continued. "That's something you and Ace have in common."

"Excuse me?" She looked up from the pot to look me directly in my face. She could see the confusion. She smiled and continued stirring the pot.

"I see he didn't tell you." she replied. "I wouldn't worry too much about it. He doesn't talk about a lot of things."

"Talk about what?" I asked.

"I'm not his biological mother." she replied.

"You're not his……" I began but was interrupted by Arsen coming into the kitchen.

"Mama! You trying to give her some lessons?" he joked.

I couldn't laugh. I was still puzzled by what his mother had just told me. Why wouldn't he tell me this? He knows everything about me. He knows everything I've been through. Why would he keep these things from me? What other secrets is he hiding? He reached to touch my shoulder, I moved over so he couldn't reach me. He could tell I was frustrated.

"Sage, you mind stepping out of the kitchen so that I can talk to my mother for a second, please?"

I wanted to tell him no. I wanted him to stop keeping secrets from me; but I didn't want to cause a scene in his mother's house. And in that moment, I knew I was too emotional to keep my cool. I sat the knife down on the counter and walked out the kitchen into the dining room. I sat down at the table with Jerod and Malachi. For a second all three of us sat around the table looking at each other, as we could vaguely hear Arsen and his "mother" speaking passionately in the kitchen.

"So Sage, you've been to Arsen's job yet?" asked Malachi. Jerod nudged him with his elbow.

"Of course I have…." I replied. "I mean, I've never actually been to his job, but we've met up a few times at the park in his work truck. He says it's dangerous for me to be on the construction sites, so I've never been." I looked up; both of them had their eyebrows raised. "What is it?" I asked, confused and frustrated. "Don't tell me he's not a construction worker either?" Neither of them would say anything, finally Jerod spoke.

"Yeah, he works in construction. Malachi here was just asking because we've never seen you up there. We all work together see."

I was slightly relieved, but a part of me felt as though they were hiding something. Like they knew something and only asked to see if I knew too. I tried to chalk all this paranoia up to the tragedy of the other night, but something wasn't right. I could feel it in my heart. Arsen walked back into the dining room.

"Malachi, can you tell the kids to come in and wash their hands?" he asked.

Malachi stood on the back porch calling for the children to come in. Lillian walked in, placing the big bowl of salad in the middle of the table. She had the plates, and silverware out already. I got up to help her bring the rest of the food into the dining room when Arsen grabbed my arm. I could tell he wanted me to sit down. "I can help her." he said walking back into the kitchen. The children ran from the bathroom into the dining room. Serenity sat down beside Malachi and Thias sat in the chair next to Arsen's seat. Arsen and his mother came back into the dining room. One holds a big mixing bowl of spaghetti noodles, and Arsen holding a bowl of sauce and a basket of rolls. They sat the bowls down and each took their place at the table. Arsen began coughing as if he was out of breath. I've noticed he has been doing that a lot lately. I rubbed his back and poured some water in his glass. He took a few sips and shook his head as if to signal that he was ok. Lillian grabbed my hand, in that second we were all holding hands and she began to bless the food.

"Father God, I come to you. I ask that you bless this family and continue to watch over each and every one of us. I thank you for our newest additions, and I pray that we continue to grow strong. Bless this food. Amen." In unison, everyone said, "Amen." We began passing the bowls around to fix our plates. I fixed Arsen and Thias's, and then passed the bowl to Lillian. There was an elephant in the room. I most definitely could tell through the silence.

"Mrs. Lillian, this is a beautiful home you have." I complimented attempting to break the ice.

"You like it? It is nice. Maybe Arsen will get you one just like it one day soon." she replied. I looked at Arsen.

"You bought your mother a house?" I said surprisingly. "That is so sweet!" I leaned over kissing him on the check. Lillian smiled, but Arsen seemed unmoved by it all. I wanted to question how he was able to do that on a construction worker budget. I mean the house was extremely big. I didn't want to put too much thought into it, I guess. I've learned in life that somethings are best when you don't know. I didn't want to ruin the moment. We all continued to talk. The atmosphere loosened up a bit, as Arsen and his brothers began to Joe on each other. Lillian eventually got up to get the apple pie she made for desert. We all had a piece. That woman can cook, everything was so fulfilling. Somehow we all migrated to the living room after a while. I snuggled up next to Arsen on the couch and listened to them as they recalled memories of each other growing up. They picked on Arsen a lot because he was the smallest. No wonder he had such a little man complex. It felt amazing to watch Thias interact and be accepted by Arsen's family; he was really enjoying himself. I still had questions that needed answers. I didn't want to believe that the man I fell in love with was the Lying King.

Chapter 10: Live Without Me

    My heart and my mind have been battling it out for days now. I didn't know what not to question. It just seemed that lately there were some things in his life that were not adding up. Why didn't he tell me he went to prison, for murder of all things? Why didn't he tell me he was adopted? What about his mother's house? That has to be close to a three hundred thousand dollar house. How was he able to afford to buy that cash as a construction worker? Why have I never actually seen where he works? Or lives, for that matter? Everything was perfect before, I just want to go back to not knowing. We are leaving for our trip to the cabins tonight. Maybe I'll bring it up then. I watch him as he walked out the store toward the car. He stood by the driver door for a second, trying to end a call before he got in the car. Finally, he opens the back door and tossed a couple of bags on the seat. I keep my eyes straight ahead as he positions himself in the front seat. Our conversation has been light for a few days. I could feel him looking at me, but I didn't budge. He sits back in his seat and rests his hands in his lap.

"Baby girl, what's on your mind?"
"If I really let out everything that was sitting on my mind, we'd both be in trouble." I thought to myself. "Nothing." I replied, keeping my conversation with him short. He leaned forward starting up and car and began driving. Silence. No music, no talking, and this time it wasn't because we were nervous from just meeting each other. No. It was the type of silence that could break mirrors. I wanted to talk about it; but I didn't want to hear the lies that I knew I would receive. I love him. How could I trust him with my life one day, and question everything in his life the next? I took someone's life to save his, to save ours; and I still don't fully understand why. Who is this man I've been giving myself too? He pulled in the parking lot of my apartment. I reached for the door, and he locks them. I unlocked my door and quickly got out, not giving him the opportunity to lock it again. I stomped my way upstairs and slamming the door behind me. He knew what was wrong, but he still acts as though nothing changed. As I sat on the bed, leaning against the headboard I could hear the front door open and close. He began walking down the hallway slowly, like a creeper. He stood at

the door with both hands down in his pants pockets.

"Are you ready to talk about it now? I want to enjoy this trip with my family tonight. I don't want us taking any unfinished business with us." he said. I continued to look straight ahead. I mean, what did he expect me to say? We were not having normal couple problems here. I KILLED someone. Someone that was trying to kill him! And if that isn't enough, I find out that he is the King of secrets, when all I wanted was him to be the King of my heart. He is acting like this is something that can be fixed in one day. "Ask me anything Sage." he continued, walking further into the room closing the door behind him. "Ask me anything and I will tell you the truth." He sat down on the bed and began taking off my shoes; throwing them on the floor and massaging my feet. I crossed both arms, staring at him. He thinks he's slick. He thinks he could just pamper me with his strong hands, and I will give up that easily. I'm not playing these games with him. I closed my eyes, leaning my head against my bed. I love his hands; the way he touches me. I opened my eyes; feeling myself growing weaken to his spell, I snatched my foot away. "Fine!" I snapped. "I have a few questions. Five to be exact; and if I feel in any way that you are lying to me, you can cancel this trip Arsen; and this relationship."

He seemed unbothered by my threats. As if he could take on this challenge and win. I wasn't playing with him though. I can walk away from this. I can walk away from him. "Where do you live?" I asked.

"Me and my brothers have a house in Decatur. I never took you there because I've been a little embarrassed, and there is no privacy." I raised my eyebrows. It seems believable. I began to loosen up a bit. "The man that you killed….why did you owe him money?"

"I technically didn't owe him money." he responded without hesitation. "We were partners. We sold dope together. One night we went to make a drop and we got robbed. He felt like I set it up because the dudes who did it were from my old neighborhood; and they shot him and not me." He looked down at my feet, picking it up again to attempt another massage. I let him. "He wanted me to prove that I didn't set it up by killing them. I couldn't do it. They were young boys; stupid, out making mistakes. I knew their mothers. I couldn't, so he felt like I was disloyal. Before I knew it, he put a hit out. People respected me. They wouldn't do it. So he did it. I killed him not only because I was angry, but I knew he would get off. His brother was lead detective."

He continued to massage my feet. I started to feel bad questioning him. Making him replay this nightmare over to satisfy my insecurities. Listening to him, the weight of pulling that trigger began to lift from my shoulders. I did what I had to, to protect us. This man would have killed me to with no hesitation.

"Next question?" he asked.

I didn't want to ask anymore question. I believed him. I trusted him again, just that quickly. "Do you know…...?" I looked up and our eyes connected. They had so much pain in them. So much hurt.

"Do I know what?" he asked.

"Do you know that I don't care about your past? You don't have to keep anything from me Arsen. I love you. I love us. I never want to lose you."

"I know Sage."

He laid my foot on the bed and got up to sit next to me. He leaned in a softly kissed my lips, while holding the side of my face. "I have one more question." I whispered, barely touching his lips with mine.

"Yes, love?"

"Do you love me?"

He leaned back to get a better view of my face, pulling my dreads back behind my ears. "I've loved you, since the moment I met you. I'll never let anything happen to you or Thias."

The front door opened and closed once more. This time it was Shelly and Thias. Shelly walks down the hallway and stands at my room door.

"Are y'all ready or what?! Can we say CABINS!!!!!" she exclaimed, excited to be taking this trip with us. Arsen looked at me to see if he had passed the test and if we were still taking this trip together as a couple.

"Girl! Our bags are packed! We were here waiting on y'all!" I said standing up grabbing a suitcase. "Oh! Shelly, Arsens brothers are going to meet us down there. I hope you don't mind?"

"Girl No! I was looking to get some action this weekend." she laughed. I just shook my head.

"I thought you were, you know?" Arsen ask Shelly.

She crossed her arms giving him the side eye. "So what? A girl can't do both?" she asked.

He smiled, shaking his head. "You do whatever makes you happy; but my brothers are savages." he laughed. "Come on y'all, let's hit the road."

We all grabbed a bag and headed for the door. Thias was already there waiting with his roller suitcase. Arsen threw all the bags in the trunk as we settled into the car. Shelly and Thias were knocked out by the time we got on the highway. I had my legs stretched out on the dashboard, one hand cuffing Arsen's. I was sure to stay up and keep him company as he was driving. We laughed and talked the entire ride. There was no pressure. No elephant. No questions. That night was no longer a factor. It was like our little secret.

We pulled up to the cabin, parking beside one of Arsen's brother cars; they left a few hours before us. I reached to the backseat to wake Shelly and Thias, as Arsen grabbed the bags out the trunk.
"We're here! Wake ya butts up!" I said nudging both of them on the knee. They slowly began to wake up. Thias's eyes lit up when he saw Malachi walking towards the car to greet Arsen. He quickly unfastened his seatbelt and jumped out the car.
"We got here quick." I laughed. "Says the broad who slept the whole ride."
Shelly tapped me on the head playfully.
"Oh, shut up! I wasn't about to stay up and be the third wheel with you two love birds." she said mocking Arsen and I. We both got out the car to head inside. It was still daylight; late evening as the sun was setting. The view was beautiful. I almost wished I had bought my canvas; this would have been a perfect moment to capture. I stood on the

deck of the porch admiring the sunset. I could hear everyone bustling around inside. Suddenly, Shelly startled me as she ran on the porch tapping my shoulder. She seemed extremely smitten. I rolled my eyes at her cheesy cat grin.

"What is it?" I asked, already knowing the answer.

"Turn around." she said grabbing my shoulders to face me toward the kitchen windows.

Arsen and his brothers were all standing in the kitchen. You could literally see everything from where we were standing. The windows of the kitchen stretched from ceiling to floor. It was absolutely beautiful. She was pointing in Malachi's direction.

"Who is that?" she asked.

"Who, Malachi?" I smiled turning back around to finish enjoying my view. "He's the middle brother. You like him?"

"I don't know about liking him Sage." she responded with a laugh. "But I sure wouldn't mind climbing that mountain for a night."

We both began to laugh. Shelly was definitely a free spirit, she didn't hold much back when it came to discussing her sexuality. She is a genuine person though. Her and I go way back and been through a lot together. She is really the only other person in this world that I trust. Malachi came out on the porch, disrupting Shelly and I's girl talk session.

"Ladies, me and the boys about to make our seafood special, y'all down?" he asked mostly looking in Shelly direction.

I smiled to myself thinking he has no idea how "down" Shelly is right now. He held out one hand to Shelly. She placed her hand in his; before walking off she looked back at me and smiled. I followed them inside, but not before taking one last look at the sunset. I sat at the island in the kitchen beside Shelly. All three men had on aprons. They were fumbling around with the pots and pans, arguing about who was going to cook what. It was quite adorable. I could see Shelly and Malachi catching each other's eye every now and then. I hadn't noticed Thias and Serenity in the living room playing the Wii. I looked back at them and smiled. This was all too perfect. I haven't felt this peaceful in a long time. Finally, Arsen snatched the apron off.

"Man y'all can have this!" he shouted, laughing at his brothers. Jerod picked up the apron and threw it at him.

"Sage, I don't know why Ace trying to act. His ass can't cook no way! Trying to show out!"

"Whatever." Arsen said smiling reaching for my hand. "My baby knows what I can do!" I took his hand and he led me upstairs to one of the oversized bedrooms. It was an amazing set up. There were rose petals on the floor and bed. And the bathroom had a glass wall with a view directly into the bedroom. He led me out onto the balcony, holding me from behind. We stood there a few moments in silence. With his arms wrapped around my waist he leaned in to kiss my neck.

"I love you Sage; but one day, you're going to have to learn to live without me. I won't always be here, but I promise I'll never leave your side."

I turned around to face him, my arms resting on his shoulders. There was a cool breeze flowing between us. The sun had already set, leaving us to stand under the light of the stars....Perfection.

"I love you Arsen. I never want to know what it feels like to live without you." I replied softly, leaning in to kiss his lips. Suddenly, gunshots broke the silence in that perfect moment, shattering the air, piercing through space one after another. Arsen grabbed my arm throwing me over the threshold of the balcony door back into the room. "Stay down!!!!" he yelled taking a gun from his right pocket and shooting in the direction of the bullets. For a few seconds they continued to exchange fire; both trying desperately to hit their mark. I couldn't think, confusion clouded my mind.

I got up to run downstairs. I had to make sure Thias was ok. By the time I had reached the bottom the shots ceased. I began to cry, frantically looking for Thias. Shelly, Serenity, and Thias were all hiding behind the couch. I ran over to them checking for marks or signs of injury. Malachi and Jerod ran back through the front door as Arsen was running down the stairs.

"Did you get him?" Arsen asked Malachi and Jerod, as the two attempted to catch their breath.

"Yeah. We got him."

"How many were there?"

"One for now. I think we should get them out of here while the road is clear." Jerod responded.

"Shit!" Arsen exclaimed sitting down on the stairs. That had been the first time I had ever heard him curse.

I got up walking towards him and raised my hand, landing it across the side of his face.

"You promised you would never put me in danger! Look at my son!!!" I yelled pointing towards Thias who was crying as Shelly held him. He stood up. I backed away scared that he would actually try to hit me back. He reached for both of my arms. "Baby...I'm sorry....I" he began.

"You what?!" I yelled. "You're a liar? You're keeping things from me? You're putting my son's life in danger? You're what!? Damnit!"

Furious, I snatched away from him to comfort Thias. He didn't respond. "We have to go, Ace." Jerod urges him to make a move.

"Who knew we were here?" he asked confused.

"Nobody but Lillian; the only explanation is that we were being followed." said Malachi.

"You call your mother, Lillian?" I asked looking at Malachi. He looks at Arsen, picking up the bags that we didn't even get to unpack.

"Malachi, take them home." Arsen demanded. "Jerod and I will stay and clean up."

I had a feeling he wasn't talking about scrubbing toilets and washing dishes. I wanted answers, but more importantly I wanted Arsen to be safe.

"I want to go home!" yelled Shelly. "I don't know what the hell kind of mafia shit y'all got going on here Sage, but I gots ta go! Ok?" She stands there with her arms crossed waiting for answers. "This that bullshit! I left the streets alone. Who the hell shoots up a damn cabin? Is it safe for me to walk outside?" she continued with her sarcastic rant.

Malachi was putting our bags in the car. Arsen walked over to me. "I'm sorry, I never meant for this to happen. I'll explain everything later." he said. I wanted to believe him. I wanted to trust him, but I couldn't. This was just too much for me to handle.

"There is no later for us, Arsen."

I grabbed Thias's hand and walked to the car where Malachi was waiting. Shelly and Serenity followed close behind. Arsen shook Malachi's hand, and they exchanged quiet words. He walked over to my window, attempting to get my attention. I continued to look straight with my arms folded. Malachi began to back out of the driveway, Arsen stood there; watching. As we headed further away from the cabin, I turned around to look at him; watching him watch us, until he was no longer in sight. Slowly, I turned around sliding down in my seat with tears silently falling from my eyes. I could see Malachi looking at me occasionally. Finally he breaks the silence and said, "My brother loves you Sage; but there are just some things you won't understand."

I rolled my eyes as the tears continued to flow. I couldn't feel the love he was talking about. At that moment all my heart felt was betrayal.

We made it back to my apartment late that night. Shelly decided to stay until the morning. I let her sleep in the bed while I lay on the couch. Something inside me was

hoping that Arsen would walk through the door. Instead my phone rang. It was him.
"Yeah."
"I didn't think you would still be up. I was going to leave a message." he said.
"Well lucky you, now you don't have to." I wanted to give in to his voice; but I couldn't let him think he could get away with hiding things from. Especially, when our life is on the line. If he hasn't figured out that he could trust me with anything by now. How could we continue on?
"Sage, I know you're upset baby girl. I called to tell you that I love you and Thias, very much; and that both of you made me a better man. I would do anything to protect you. I wish I could change what happen ton……"
There was silence. I looked at my phone to see that the call had dropped. I dialed his number attempting to call back. It went straight to voicemail. I tried once more….nothing. I lay down on the couch with the phone in my hand. I wanted to make sure I could hear it when he called back while I was sleeping. I clutched the phone tight, waiting for it to ring; until I fell asleep. It never did.

Chapter 11:
Disappearing Acts

It's been two weeks since the shootout at the cabin. I haven't heard from Arsen since. I know I told him it was over, but I didn't actually expect him to let us go that easily. Thias's grandparents practically begged me to let him stay for the summer. I had never been away from him that long, but he needs to spend time with that side of his family. Florida is too far way. Besides, that would give me some alone time to figure things out with Arsen. That's the thing though, since Thias has been gone all I've had was alone time. Not knowing is what irks my soul. I mean he hasn't even called to tell me he was ok or I'm sorry can we work it out, nothing! It's like I didn't even exist. I have been pacing back and forth in my apartment for weeks. I considered popping up at "his" house but I don't even know where that is. I never paid attention to the fact that we were always at my house, or that I never really knew where he worked. Those things seemed unimportant when we were together all the time. What else could I have possibly needed to know? My phone started to ring. I ran to hoping it was Arsen, but knowing it wasn't by the ringtone.

Maybe he's calling from a different number.
I didn't have this number saved in my phone.
"Hello?"

"Sage, this is Lillian. Arsen's mother." she
said. Her voice was a bit shaky like she had
been crying.

"Have you heard from Arsen? I haven't
spoken to him or seen him in two weeks. I
know we got into an argu........"

"Sage! Please. We need to talk. I'm only
calling you because I know this is what he
would have wanted. "She was referring to
him in past tense, as if he was no longer here
or something. I didn't understand.

"What he would have wanted?" I repeated.
"I don't understand."

"You should meet me at Grady." she said,
hanging up the phone.

I called Shelly to have her pick me up and
take me to Grady. I couldn't explain
anything to her because I didn't know
myself. I just know the whole ride there my
heart was beating fast and I tried not to think
the worst. Lillian told me to meet her on the
third floor but she didn't give me a room
number. Shelly and I get on the elevator to
the third floor. As it began to move I could
feel my heart sinking to the pit of my
stomach. Seeing the discomfort in my face,
Shelly reached over and grabbed my hand.
The elevator stopped. We made it. It seemed
like it took forever for the doors to open. As

we stepped off I looked to the left, and then to the right. I was unsure which way to go, as Lillian refused to give me the correct room number. I just wanted to see him; to let him know that it is ok, I forgive him. I love him. I look ahead and Lillian and Jerod are walking toward us. The look on their face said it all.

"Sage, I know he didn't tell you; but I want you to not dwell on the fact that he didn't tell you and try to understand the why." she began. I gripped Shelly's hand tighter, attempting to brace myself for whatever was coming next. My lips couldn't move and her voice sounded as if I was listening to her speak from under water. "Ace, had brain cancer." she continued. My heart fell even further inside me. "He stopped getting treatment and was preparing for whatever the consequences would be. He knew....." she paused looking back at Jerod. He nodded giving her the ok to continue. "He knew he would eventually die."

"So what the hell are you saying?" Shelly yelled.

Lillian cut her eyes at Shelly and then back at me; throwing her hands up as if she was through with this conversation and walking back towards the waiting room. I looked at Jerod.

"Please, don't tell me….." I said staring
Jerod in his eyes. He couldn't look at me as
he began to speak.
"He's gone Sage. He passed away this
morning."
Nothing could have prepared me for this
moment. It was like my heart had just been
ripped out of my chest repeatedly. I felt my
legs collapsed up under me. Before I knew
it, I was on the floor; tears flowing like a
broken dam. I couldn't catch my breath and
my head began throbbing. I could feel
Shelly behind me trying to hold me up. I felt
robbed; robbed of my happiness, of my love,
of my last moments with him. I didn't get to
say goodbye.
"I don't understand!" I muffled between my
heart wrenching cry. "I want to see him. I
need to see him! I want to see my
baby…….." I yelled as I scrambled to get to
my feet but I could barely feel my legs.
"Where is he?" I began to crawl down the
hallway. "Where is he?!! I want to know."
I couldn't see through my locs. Jerod picks
me up from the floor. I began to kick for
him to put me down. "I want to see him,
please just let me see him." I yelled.
Nobody was listening. My voice began to go
horse, I had cried so loud. As Jerod held me,
I could see Shelly trying to get the elevator
opened as she fought back tears. "I'm not

leaving until I see him! Please! Please let me see him." I begged.

Jerod could no longer hold me. I slid to the floor and he kneeled down beside me rubbing my back. "He's not here Sage....I'm sorry." he said trying to soothe me. I could hear the bell of the elevator signaling that it had made it to our floor. Shelly reached for my arm and Jerod grabbed the other pulling me up to my feet and helping me onto the elevator. I was slumped over with my head down. The only thing keeping me up was Shelly and Jerod on either side of me.

"I don't understand... I don't understand... I just don't understand. God please.....Why?" I began to get dizzy. My world had just been turned upside down. How could this be? How could this end so soon. I thought we were going to spend the rest of our lives together. He was my everything. I was on an emotional roller coaster with a million unanswered questions.

Eventually, we made it to the car. They put me in the passenger seat and I sat there as Jerod spoke with Shelly for what seemed like forever. The minutes seemed to pass by like hours. Shelly made her way back into the car. Before driving off she reached over; stoking my dreads trying to wipe the tears from my face. I began mumbling through my cries as if I were trying to talk to myself.

"Sage. Hunny, I am so sorry. I am so sorry."
My heart felt heavy. I know she was trying
to comfort me but I couldn't hold my head
up to acknowledge her.

"He promised me. He promised me....he
would never leave me. He promised me."
By the time we made it back to my
apartment I had cried so much for so long,
my eyes had swollen. I couldn't see, and I
could barely talk.

"I'm going to spend the night with you. I
don't want you by yourself." she said
guiding me up the stairs to my apartment. I
dragged myself down the hallway to my
room, still whimpering like a lost puppy. I
lay down across my bed. Shelly came in
behind me, pulling my shoes off and turning
off the lights. She didn't say anything. I
knew she didn't have the words to say. She
lay down next to me, lifting my head into
her arms, patting me on my back softly to
comfort me. I held on to her crying into her
shoulder. I cried for him. I cried for him all
night, but he never came.

Chapter 12: Pity Party

I stayed in bed for days. I couldn't eat and barely got up to wash my ass. I had a stench to me, but I didn't care. Nothing mattered to me anymore, except Thias. I didn't want to tell him while he was in Florida. I didn't want to ruin his trip. If he knew I was here alone, he would want to come home and I didn't want that for him. I wanted him happy. Whenever he would call I was sure to lift my spirits so he couldn't tell that anything was bothering me. I wasn't entirely sure how I would break the news to him anyway. I wanted to prolong it as much as possible. I knew I would have to face it sooner than later; but I would rather later than now. He had another month before it was time for him to come back. I, on the other hand, was trying to figure out a way to cope with my extremely unwanted reality. Arsen. He kept so much from me. His mother asked me to understand why. Lord knows I have been trying. I should have been there. I should have been by his side. He should have let me decide, but instead he made that decision for me. He thought he knew what was best for me but he didn't. I should have been there, and now I have to live with the fact that I wasn't., and I never got to say goodbye.

My body was beginning to feel weak. I could tell I was shutting down. I haven't eaten in days. I've tried to find the energy to get up and cook but I didn't have it. I even thought about praying, but my pain wouldn't allow me to do that either. I'm trying not to understand why life is the way it is, because I know it's not for me to know. But I don't know what I believe anymore. I've been through so much, and I was finally happy. I was finally free. I couldn't help but think that it's because of that night; this is my karma, I thought. It has to be. I didn't know what hurt worst; losing Arsen or feeling like it's my fault he is gone. I thought God understood. I thought all was forgiven in the universe. I guess not.

My head was buried so far under my covers that I hadn't notice someone knocking on my door. The knocks were relentless. Almost as if whoever knew I was here and was not leaving until I decided to answer the door. I dragged myself from the bed down the hallway to the door, covered in nothing but a robe and musk stemming from my armpits. I unlocked the door. Not even checking to see who was on the other side. Probably Shelly. Most likely coming to check on me because I haven't been answering her calls or anyone else's for that matter. There stood Lillian and Malachi. Shocked I grabbed the ends of my robe, securing the belt around me to cover up. Lillian looked me up and down before stepping in as Malachi followed.

"I bought you this." she said handing me what seemed to be a vase.

"It's an urn. Ace didn't want a funeral he wanted to be cremated. Those were his wishes." she continued with a sign, scoping out my apartment, judging with her eyes. I grabbed the vase holding it not sure where I was supposed to place it.

"If you guys would excuse me." I said taking the vase with Arsen's ashes into my room. I wasn't back there long when Lillian made her way to my bedroom door.

"Those are very nice paintings, Sage. You did those yourself?" I looked around my room at all the paintings. Each one representing some type of memory I had shared with Arsen. It seemed like my best work was when I was able to reflect on moments of love and happiness.

"I did." I replied.

"And that one there....." she said pointing at one of my paintings walking further into my room. "Is that Arsen?"

"Yes it is."

"Sage, I came over here to check on you. To make sure you were alright. Ace made it very clear how he felt about you. So his brothers and I will make it a point to make sure you and your son is well. Have you eaten?" she asked.

My face had begun to get pale and my lips dry and cracked over these past few days. All I've been doing is crying and sleeping. My heart wouldn't allow room for anything else.

"No." I replied, sitting down on the edge of my bed.

"I didn't come over here to give you a pity party....." she began. "I came to give you the explanation that I know your heart needs." She sat on the bed beside me placing her hand over my knee. Old people use that same gesture every time they are about to tell you something you might not want to hear. "Ace knew he was dying when he met you. He made the decision that you and your son is who he wanted to spend his last days with. He didn't tell you because he didn't want you to be sad. He didn't want to remember you that way."

"Well doesn't that make him selfish?" I asked. "He took away my option, when he decided not to tell me. Don't I get to choose whether I want to deal with this type of pain or not? Shouldn't I have a say in that? I thought we were going to spend the rest of our lives together....."

"Oh Sage....." She stood up pacing around my room looking at each picture I had on display. "But you did spend the rest of his life with him."

Becoming increasingly frustrated with her optimistic attitude about the situation, I stood up with her placing both hands on my hips. "He lied to me! Period! And he left me here to face the truth alone! I fell in love with a man that knew he couldn't spend the rest of his life with me!" My voice began to crack as I tried hard to fight back the tears. "He knew! And yet he promised me everything he couldn't give me! I didn't get to say good bye! Not at the hospital! Not at a funeral! Hell, not even at a damn ceremony!!! I didn't get to tell him that I love him....." I fell to my knees covering my face with both hands sobbing at my pain. "I didn't know who he was with all his secrets, Lillian. I fell in love with a stranger."

"Sometimes Sage that is the best love to fall into." she said slightly smiling. I was sick of her riddles. I couldn't understand how she was so calm.

"And quite honestly, if that is what you were worried about, I promise you will learn all you need to know about Ace through his death. You just have to be patient."

I looked up at her confused. I noticed she liked to talk in circles. Never actually saying what it is she should say.

"Be patient?" I asked. "I'm supposed to be patient. I killed someone trying to protect him and he knew he was going to die anyway!!!" I yelled out of anger.

Shocked that I had just confessed to murder, I placed my hand over my mouth; wishing that I had more control over my emotions in that moment and could take back everything I had just said. Lillian seemed unbothered by my statement, as if she already knew.

"One thing about my son; when he says he is going to handle something, he handles it. Despite what you may be feeling right now Sage, you have no worries."

She began to walk out my room toward the front door where Malachi stood waiting. He hadn't moved since they got here, almost like he was her bodyguard. I followed behind her hoping she would leave. I couldn't have company right now, and I definitely couldn't entertain someone who wanted so badly for me to understand a reason for this all. Before walking out the door, she turned and looked at me, fiddling with the straps of her purse she was holding. "Sage, death is a beautiful part of life. You have to embrace it. It's a chance for our soul to get a fresh start. We never really die, you know?" she said. "And please, eat something. Take care of yourself. Don't starve my grandbaby." "Excuse me?" I wasn't sure if she was calling me fat or what; but I had definitely had enough of her mouth at this point. "I'm not pregnant, Lillian." She raised her eyebrows and smiled; patting Malachi on the shoulders as if to signal him to open the door. Without saying another word she walked out, Malachi nodded and followed close behind. I locked the door leaning against it for a second before sliding myself to the floor, trying to absorb the ridiculousness that had just occurred. I'm not sure if I like her much. I'm not sure of anything these days, it seems.

Chapter 13: The Gift

It had only been about three weeks since Arsen's death, and I had been getting sicker by the day. I had been trying to pull myself together as Thias was coming home the following week. I still hadn't figured out how I would tell him. I know how much he loved Arsen. My house was beginning to look like a dump. I hadn't washed clothes in weeks or dishes for that matter. I just laid there buried under my pillows and blankets. I could hear Shelly clacking around in the kitchen and living room attempting to clean up a bit. She had been coming over every day to check on me. Eventually, she took my key so she wouldn't have to stand at the door knocking; waiting for me to let her in. I haven't been outside since I left the hospital that day. I knew I would have to get it together soon. I have to show Thias that I am strong; although, I question my strength a lot lately. Shelly began tapping on my bedroom door.

"You have to get up, Sage. Put on some clothes." she demanded.

"What for?"

"Listen, Malachi asked me to have you meet up with Lillian at some lawyer's office."

"I'm not going." I said pushing myself deeper under the covers.

She had enough of my behavior at this point. She snatched the covers off me and began raiding my closet for an outfit. She threw a sundress on my bed. It was the same one I had worn to Arsen's family dinner. Everything reminded me of him.

"I'm not going to let you do this to yourself. I tried to let you work through this your way; but I be damned if I'm going to sit here and watch you kill yourself." I sat up in the bed using my elbows to hold me up. She was serious. "You have twenty minutes to bathe and put this dress on or I'm coming back here to do it for you." she demanded with her hands on her hips. She walked out my room slamming the door behind me.

She was right. I couldn't allow myself to die too. I pushed myself onto my feet and into the shower. The hot water felt good over my body. I could barely stand as my body had been weak. I still haven't eaten much. I quickly turned the water off and stepped out the shower as I could feel myself no longer able to stand. I sat down on the toilet seat to dry off, glad that I had bathed for the first time in weeks. I didn't bother staring into the mirror as I usually do. I just slip on my bra, panties, and dressed before walking down the hallway. When Shelly saw me, her eyes lit up. She quickly ran over to hug me.

"You ready?" she asked. Shrugging my shoulders I agreed. She handed me a cup with a banana smoothie she had just whipped up for me in the kitchen. I didn't want to reject it. I knew she was trying to make me feel better. She opened the front door for me, and as soon as I step out the summer breeze hit my face. I felt like I had been in prison and I was experiencing my first moment as a free woman. My legs were still numb. Shelly had to help me down the stairs and into her car. I stared out the window, wishing that my life was different. At one point, Shelly had gotten lost. I could hear Malachi on the phone trying to give her directions. Finally, we made it to a parking garage off Hurtz street downtown. Shelly drove up a couple of floors until we found a parking space. I had been sipping on that smoothie she gave me and it seemed to give me a bit of energy. She helped me out the car and onto the elevator which opened up to the inside of an office building. As we turned the corner I could see Lillian, Malachi, and Jerod standing there anticipating our arrival. The closer we got to them the more my stomach began to turn. What are we here for? I hope she don't expect me to confess to a lawyer. Why else would she have me up here like this? I walked up to Lillian.

"What is this about?" I asked scared out of my mind. She smiled, embracing me around my shoulders guiding me into the lawyer's office.

"I told you Sage, you have no worries."

This damn woman. Something was off in her mind, it had to be. We continued to walk into what seemed to be a conference room. A very well dressed white man came in behind us with a hand full of vanilla folders. We all took a seat, Lillian being sure to sit next to me. He stood at the head of the table, folding his hands in front of him.

"We are all here today to read the will of Mr. Robinson, I presume?" he asked.

Arsen's brother and his mother shook their head in agreement. Hell. I wasn't sure what I was doing here. I'm almost positive Arsen left nothing in his will for me and I am even more certain that I didn't want anything either.

"Really, Ms. Williams is actually the only one who hasn't given her signature." he said flipping through one of the folders in front of him. "Ms. WIlliams." he began. "If you could please hand me your I.D., I just need to make sure your identification matches with what I have on the will."

I fumbled through my purse. I couldn't get a good grip of my I.D because my hands wouldn't stop shaking. Lillian reached over to assist, handing the lawyer my I.D. He looked at it, and then at me, and then back at his folder.

"Ok, Mr. Robinson left to you this…" he said sliding a white envelope across the table with an address on it. I picked it up to examine it. It was sealed and I could feel at least two keys in it. *"It must be the keys to his half of the house he shared with his brothers…"* I thought to myself. *"….If that was even the truth."*

"He also left you……" he continued gathering a few documents stacking them neatly to hand to me. "The funds in his checking account that totals to about five hundred……..thousand dollars." he said sliding the paperwork over to me.

My heart dropped. I stood up leaving the envelope and the papers on the table. I looked around the room and everyone was smiling at me. I was confused.

"I can't accept that. Why didn't he leave it to his mother?" I asked.

"Because he wanted to make sure you had no worries, for goodness sake Sage. I don't need the money." she said shaking her head.

"I can't…." I said as I ran out of the conference room. I had to catch my breath, I was so overwhelmed, and I felt like I was suffocating in there. Jerod stepped out behind me.

"Sage, take the money. He knew what he was doing. Let him do it."

"This isn't what I want, Jerod. I don't want to be here. I want him here. I want the truth. Money can't change the fact that my heart is broken."

Lillian comes from the door as she was listening to our conversation. "Sage, the money is yours. The account is there. You don't have to touch it if you don't want to, but please take the keys." she begged handing me the envelope I had left on the table. "Sign the paper, take the keys. The money is there whether you want it or not." she said as she walked back into the conference room.

I followed her in and attempted to sign the paperwork; but my hands would not stop shaking. I looked up to Shelly for her assistance. She began to guide my hands helping me sign my name. I folded the envelope down inside my purse. Shelly helped me out into the hallway and back into the elevator as Lillian finished speaking with the lawyers. I was so overwhelmed, by the time we got back to my apartment all I wanted to do was sleep. I sat on the edge of my bed pulling the envelope out of my purse looking at the address. It seemed so familiar but I was too tired to think. I threw it on my night stand, burying myself back under the covers; drifting back into another deep, depressing, sleep.

Chapter 14: His Last Goodbye

The next week wasn't much different from my last. I was anticipating Thias coming home. Shelly went to pick him up for me. I had gotten up that morning to clean. I didn't want him to see how I had been living these past few weeks without him. I even tried to eat something, but everything I put to my mouth made me nauseous. I went weeks without eating a full meal, now I couldn't keep anything down. I had never felt this type of pain or been through a depression like this before. I had been through so much but losing someone I love, just took too much out of me. I managed to straighten up my room a bit, tossing clothes from one corner to the other. I was completely drained. I sat on the side of my bed to catch my breath when I heard the door close and Thias running down the hallway. He ran in my room jumped on the bed and wrapped his arms around me holding me tight.

"Mama, he's coming back. Don't worry." he said.

I could only assume he was talking about Arsen. I began to pat him on the back as I watched Shelly walk into the room.

"I'm sorry Sage, he was asking questions. I had to tell him." she said.

It was ok. I'm glad she did, because I still hadn't figured out a way to do it myself.

"Baby…." I said rubbing the back of his head. "He is not coming back love; he is in Heaven now, with God."

He pushes back from me, tears building up in his eyes as if he couldn't believe what I was telling him.

"No Mama! He is! I know he is!" he cried.

"Listen to me Thias! He's not, ok? He's just not!" I yelled at him.

I didn't mean to, but it was hurting me. He wanted to believe things would change when I knew they wouldn't. He swung his bag around knocking everything on my nightstand to the floor and ran out the room. I could hear his room door slam. Tears began to form in my eyes as I slid off the bed to pick my things up off the floor. Shelly kneeled down to help me.

"I'm sorry." she said. She didn't need to apologize. I appreciate her for everything. I just barely knew how to handle my hurt, and now I have to comfort Thias in his. She picked up the envelope with the keys in it.

"Let's go Sage." she said with excitement in her voice.

"What?"

"Let's get y'all out the house. Let's go see what door this key opens. You had it for a week. You're not at all curious." I grabbed the envelope out her hand staring at the address.

"Ok, let's go." I agreed. She jumped up running to Thias's room to see if he was ok. I got up and slipped on a pair of Arsen's baller shorts that was left at my house and a t-shirt.

By the time we all got into Shelly's car, there was a sense of adventure running through all three of us. She entered the address into her GPS, and we spent the next twenty minutes trying to guess what we were going to see when we got there. It was some place downtown. Shelly began to make some familiar turns.

"I've been this way before." I said. "I just can't remember what for."

She continued driving making a left and then another right. Suddenly, the GPS signaled that we had arrived at our destination.

Shelly pulled up slowly unsure of which building we should go to; but when I saw it, I knew. I flung open the car door before Shelly put the car in park; stumbling to my feet as my legs had gotten weak. *"I can't believe he did this."* I thought to myself. I tried to rip open the envelope but my hands were shaking. I was nervous, excited, and sad all at the same time. I could hear the car doors open and shut behind me. "Well Mama, what is this place?" Thias asked.

I almost had the envelope open when both keys fell to the ground. Shelly leaned over to pick them up.

"Which building is it Sage?" she asked. "I don't see any numbers."

"It's that one. That door right there." I said pointing to the same store front that I was admiring months ago.

"Well, how do you know?" she asked uncertainly.

"Shelly I told him that this is the building I wanted for my gallery and he bought it. I can't believe he bought it!"

She walked up to the door and pushed in the first key. Thias and I stood back in anticipation. She jiggled the door but it wouldn't move. "I don't think this is it, girl!"

"Just try the other key Shelly." I encouraged her.

She switched keys, attempting to jiggle the handle once more. The lock popped and the door pushed opened. We both started screaming, jumping up and down; exchanging hugs with excitement. Thias ran past us pushing his way into the gallery first.

"Oh Mama! This is cool! You finally got your gallery!!!"

We all looked around in amazement. It was a nice size space. Thias was talking so loud you could hear his voice echoing; as the floors were concrete. "This is amazing Sage. This is going to be so beautiful." I began to cry. I tried to hold back; but I just couldn't believe that he did all this for me. In his last days he thought of me and my future. I closed my eyes taking in a deep breath. The smell of the fresh paint immediately went to my head. I turned around to admire the view of the display window, imagining which paintings I would sit there. Shelly and Thias were behind me exploring the place. As I stood there my eyes caught a glimpse of a figure standing across the street, staring into the window looking at me. I squint my eyes a bit to get a better view of the face. Then he smiled, showing all his gold teeth. I closed my eyes telling myself that there is no way I could be looking at Arsen. When I opened them, he was gone. He had disappeared or maybe he was never there to begin with. I don't know, but what I do know is I missed him so much. "So what are you going to name it?" Shelly asked.

"What?" I asked.

"What? The gallery...duh girl! What you over there thinking about?" she laughed.

"Oh, I haven't thought about it Shelly. Hell I didn't know I had one until ten minutes ago." I laughed.

"Mama! How about this?" Thias asked walking from the back holding a card in his hand.

"Where this come from?" I asked.

"I found it on the table back there."

It was a postcard. On one side it had a picture of Thias, Arsen and I. On the other it read, "Ace of Sage". "Ace of Sage." I read aloud. "I like that.....Ace of Sage Art Gallery. What y'all think?"

Shelly raised her hand to give me a high five. "I love it! I love it!!!!" she yelled.

"Me too Mama." agreed Thias.

We all began to hug and laugh, our hearts were light. We spent a few moments discussing designs and decorations. Suddenly, the front door opened causing the bells hanging over to ring. We all jumped to look towards the door as we were not expecting any company.

"Well, she is not officially opened for business, but we would definitely like to help you out." Shelly said in a flirtatious way offering services as if she was my assistant. She knew she had the job anyway.

"No need. Unfortunately, I'm not here for that type of business matter." he said still standing by the door with his hands crossed in front of him. I had never seen him before and wasn't really sure what he wanted. I couldn't help but notice how well dressed he was. He wore black slacks and polo like shirt. I couldn't make out the print that was on the corner of his shirt. He was standing too far from me. He had what seemed to be a military watch on his right arm. Clean cut, medium height, and dark skinned.

"I'm not sure if we would be much help to you, Sir. I mean we literally just found out that we own this building." I explained.

"Ms. Sage Williams?" he asked.

His tone of voice made me nervous. My stomach began to knot up, but I managed to answer him. "Yes, how can I help you?"

"My name is Victor Johnson. I am the lead detective assigned to the missing person's case of my fellow colleague, Ahmad Carrington."

My heart felt like it had stopped. My past had come back to haunt me; but I couldn't break, not in front of Thias.

"Mr. Johnson, I'm not sure how I can help you. I'm sorry but I don't even know who that is." I replied trying to hold my composure and make my lie believable.

"Miss Williams, I believe you can help me, you see? Your recently deceased companion knew him very well." he said as his eyes pierced through mine. Shelly could see that I wasn't feeling good. She ran for the trashcan by the door, and just as she brought it to me I began to vomit.

"Listen, Victor…" she began as she was holding my dreads out the way of the trashcan. "She just lost the love of her life and she hasn't been feeling well lately. This is her first time out the house in weeks. I'm sure you can find other people in Atlanta who actually know your friend." He uncrossed his hands; never taking his eyes off me, even as Shelly was talking to him. "Miss Williams." he continued. "I intend to find out what happened to this detective. I'll come visit you again when you're feeling better." he said almost as if he knew I was the answer to all his questions. "You all have a good day; and congratulations on your new business Miss Williams." he said as he walked back out the door causing the bells to ring once more. I watched him drive off in his dark blue Crown Vic.

TRUE GLORY PUBLICATIONS

IF YOU WOULD LIKE TO BE A PART OF OUR TEAM, PLEASE SEND YOUR SUBMISSIONS BY EMAIL TO TRUEGLORYPUBLICATIONS@GMAIL.COM. PLEASE INCLUDE A BRIEF BIO, A SYNOPSIS OF THE BOOK, AND THE FIRST THREE CHAPTERS. SUBMIT USING MICROSOFT WORD WITH FONT IN 11 TIMES NEW ROMAN.

Check out these other great books from True Glory Publications
A Child Of a Crackhead

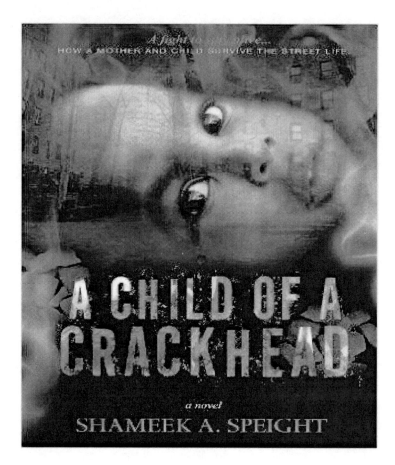

A Crazy Ghetto Love Story

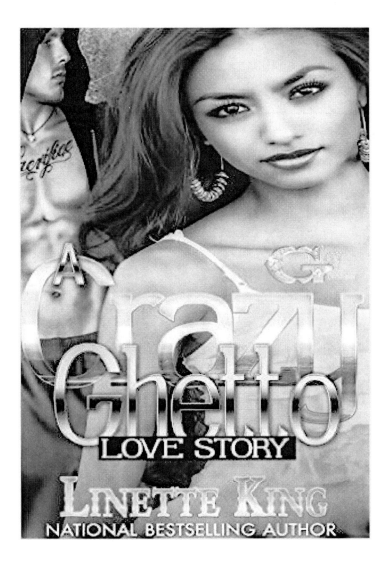

A Crazy Ghetto LOVE STORY

LINETTE KING

NATIONAL BESTSELLING AUTHOR

CPSIA information can be obtained at www.ICGtesting.com
Printed in the USA
LVOW10s1758110416

483082LV00018B/1204/P

9 781530 822454